CLASSIC Nasty

ALSO BY JACK MURNIGHAN

The Naughty Bits

Full Frontal Fiction (coeditor)

CLASSIC

Nasty

more **NAUGHTY BITS:**

a **ROLLICKING GUIDE** *to* **HOT SEX IN GREAT BOOKS,**

from **THE ILIAD** *to* **THE CORRECTIONS**

JACK MURNIGHAN

FOUR WALLS EIGHT WINDOWS

NEW YORK / LONDON

Published in the United States by
Four Walls Eight Windows
39 West 14th Street
New York, NY 10011
http://www.4w8w.com

First printing July 2003.

Library of Congress Cataloging-in-Publication Data
Murnighan, Jack.
    Classic nasty : more naughty bits, a rollicking guide to hot sex in great books, from The Iliad
    to The Corrections / Jack Murnighan.
        p. cm.
    ISBN: 1-56858-250-1 (trade pbk.)
    1. Sex—Literary collections. I. Title.

    PN6071.S416 M868 2003
    808.8′03538—dc21   2002192750

Pages 205–207 represent an extension of the copyright page.

10 9 8 7 6 5 4 3 2 1

Printed in Canada

Book design by Sara E. Stemen

To Erik and Hillary,
since I had so much trouble saying it at the wedding...

CONTENTS

What is pornography to one man is the laughter of genius to another.

——D. H. LAWRENCE

INTRODUCTION

Over the four years that I wrote my Nerve.com column "Jack's Naughty Bits," I began and ended with a few lines from Dante's *Inferno* that I thought encapsulated perfectly everything the naughty bits was about. The scene is Dante's famous encounter with Paolo and Francesca, the couple who went to hell for an adulterous love spurred on by reading a racy book. As Francesca grudgingly tells Dante, she and Paolo were in love, stolen away in a secluded grove, unseen by prying eyes, hand in hand under a tree, *reading*. At a certain moment, the book turned a little steamy, they looked at each other, Paolo kissed her, the book was dropped, and no more did they read that day. And now, for their sin, they find themselves in especially warm climes for eternity,

Paolo and Francesca's story dramatizes the power I've always thought books should possess: to move, to stir the senses, to elicit thoughts, feelings, moods, memories and even illicit kisses from one's secret paramour. Perhaps now in our age of images and Internet it's difficult to imagine; we are much more likely to lean over and smooch our beloved in the dim lights of the cinema than hand in hand over the same book. (I mean, I read a lot, but while doing so am I not typically, tragically, alone?) But the power that Francesca is describing remains, and that's why I've compiled this second volume of great naughty bits. We read to feel, and I hope some of these bits help you feel as much as Francesca.

from Dante's INFERNO

> ... There is no greater pain
> Than to remember happy days in days
> Of sadness ...

But if to know the first root of our love
You have so strong a desire,
I'll do as one who weeps while he speaks.

One day, for pleasure simply, we were reading
Of Lancelot, and how love overpowered him;
Alone we were, and free from all suspicions.

Often that reading caused our eyes to meet,
And often the color from our faces went,
But it was a single passage that overcame us:

When we read how the desired smile was
Kissed by one so true a lover, this one,
Who from me will never be taken,

Kissed me, his body all trembling, on the mouth.
...And no more did we read that day.

—TRANSLATED BY JACK MURNIGHAN

ong live transportation sex. Mile-high lavatory love, greased-rail train sex, backseat cab coitus, hummers while driving (even if you're driving a Hummer) and, my personal favorite, the eight-and-a-half-foot club (sex in a Greyhound bus). It's clear that moving vehicle violations are a potent pool for sexual adventure—something about the combination of burning fossil fuels, vibrating machinery and the risk of getting caught adds to sexual frisson like little else. However many pistons are pumping, people love sex on the move—or at least they love fantasizing about it. Sad truth is, the reality often disappoints. (One friend was interrupted in his mile-high triumph by the pounding of flight attendants on the door; while *in flagrante*, his back seems to have been pressed against the steward call button!) But if you can find a cabbie who will take your hundred-dollar tip and keep his eyes on the road, or a fellow insomniac to slip into the loo while the rest of the bus riders are counting sugarplums or, dream of dreams, a cabinmate on an international train with whom the only language you share is the kiss—then, my friends, you have the stuff of stories. Or at least the stuff of bad fiction.

Now why would I use "bad fiction" as my setup to segue into a discussion of that consummate work of '60s French erotica, *Emmanuelle*? Normally my erotica cheese limit is easily reached, and I can only see the female genitalia described as "the sex" so many times before wincing commences. But, alas, if any work rivals Erica Jong's *Fear of Flying* for most famous transportation sex scene, it is certainly the opening airplane adventure of young Emmanuelle. Though most people will remember the scene from the movie and not the book (from which it differs substantially), Emmanuelle on the page exhibits the same groundless, spontaneous, indiscriminate sexual lashing-out that erotica readers (and viewers) seem to want in a woman. So here she is, the great icon of female sexual liberation (at least for men), the notorious Emmanuelle...

from *Emmanuelle Arsan's* EMMANUELLE

Emmanuelle boarded the plane in London that was to take her to Bangkok... The steward led her to her seat. It was what would normally have been a window seat, but there was no window. She could see nothing beyond the draped walls. It made no difference to her. She did not care about anything but abandoning herself to the powers of that deep seat, drifting into drowsiness between its wooly arms, against its foam shoulder, on its long, mermaid lap...

The steady, subdued, almost imperceptible vibrations of the metal fuselage attuned her body to the frequency. Starting from her knees, a wave rose along her thighs, resonating on the surface, moving higher and higher, making her quiver... Thinking Emmanuelle was asleep, the stewardess cautiously tilted back her seat, transforming it into a bed, and spread a cashmere blanket over her long, languid legs... Emmanuelle had abandoned herself to the stewardess's care without opening her eyes. Her reverie, however, had lost none of its intensity or urgency. Her right hand now began to move over her belly, very slowly, restraining itself, descending toward her pubis. The thin blanket undulated above it. Her finger tips, pushing down on the soft silk of her skirt, whose narrowness made it difficult for her to spread her legs, found the bud of flesh in erection that they sought and pressed it tenderly. Her middle finger began the gentle, careful motion that would bring on orgasm. Almost immediately, [a] man's hand came down on hers...

The man's hand did not move. Merely by its weight, it applied pressure to her clitoris, on which her hand was resting.

Nothing else happened for some time. She then became aware that his other hand was lifting the blanket and drawing it aside. It took hold of her knee and felt its curves and hollows. It rose slowly along her thigh and soon passed over the top of her stocking.

When it touched her bare skin, she started for the first time and tried to break the spell. She sat up awkwardly and turned halfway on her side. As though they wanted to punish her for her futile revolt, the man's hands abandoned her abruptly. But before she had time to react, they were on her again, this time at her waist. They deftly unfastened and unzipped her skirt, pulled it down to her knees, then moved up again. One of them slipped under her panties and caressed her flat, muscular belly, just above the high mound of her pubis, stroking it as though it were the neck of a thoroughbred... Then the hand forced her thighs to spread further apart. It closed over her warm, swollen sex, caressing it as if to soothe it, without haste, following the furrow of its lips, dipping in lightly between them, passing over her erect clitoris and coming to rest on the thick curls of her pubis. As they moved to and fro between her legs, the fingers sank deeper between her moist membranes, slowing their advance, and seeming to hesitate as her tension increased. Biting her lips to stifle the sob that was rising from her throat, she panted with desire as the man brought her closer and closer to orgasm without letting her reach it...

A buzzing sound indicated the loudspeaker was about to be used. The stewardess's voice, deliberately softened so the passengers would not be awakened too abruptly, announced that the plane would land at Bahrein in about twenty minutes.

—TRANSLATED BY LOWELL BAIR

on IN PRAISE OF THE STEPMOTHER

MARIO VARGAS LLOSA

od, it is said, is in the details. It is a curse of consciousness that, in order to be able to process the data of everything that happens around us—whether daily and dull, or as in recent years, chaotic in the extreme—we must filter away much of each moment's teeming nuance. To understand the things of this world, we must focus on similarities and, in doing so, eradicate many of the differences. To assimilate, to collate, we must ignore. This is why God is in the details, because to register them, to be able to appreciate the smallest of life's miracles, we need give pause, unhinge our reason, let our consciousness be less human—and thereby more divine. Nietzsche famously described the basic process of language (and of philosophy) as the ability to take any number of disparate entities and refer to them all as one thing. By this process, we come to understand them, in a certain sense. That mass of objects, those are "leaves," whatever their differences. But the reverse process, to take a pile of leaves and be able to separate them out—this one burnished, this torn, this prominently reticulate—brings the uniqueness, the great miracle of individuality, into full view. To live in the world we must see patterns, but to feel the full weight of this pendant globe we must strive to see the uniqueness of its elements. The magic is in the being of each thing, each and every time.

All of this is better shown than said, of course, and better demonstrated than explained. I'm therefore going to excerpt a passage from Mario Vargas Llosa's supremely sensual and philosophical novel *In Praise of the Stepmother*. I'm picking one representative of the book's central vein: the great Don Rigoberto's affection for the all and everything of his wife, Lucrecia. Rigoberto loves his wife, and will always love her, all at once and piece by piece. Rigoberto sees and feels with lucidity that anything associated with Lucrecia is part of her, and consequently worthy of love (and libidinal association). How does this relate

to the God of details? Because, at base, when Rigoberto sees each detail of his beloved he says to himself, over and over, *This is you. This is you.* **And therein lies the enduring wonder.**

from Mario Vargas Llosa's IN PRAISE OF THE STEPMOTHER

As he rolled little balls of cotton around the tips of the tweezers and wet them with soap and water so as to clean out the wax that had accumulated inside his ear, he anticipated what those clean funnels would soon be hearing as they descended from his wife's breasts to her navel. They need make no special effort there to surprise Lucrecia's secret music, for a veritable symphony of sounds, liquid and solid, prolonged and brief, diffuse and clear, would immediately reveal their hidden life to him. He looked forward with gratitude to how deeply he would be moved to perceive, thanks to those organs which he was now scraping clean with meticulous care and affection, ridding them of the oily film that formed on them every so often, something of the secret existence of her body: glands, muscles, blood vessels, hair follicles, membranes, tissues, filaments, ducts, tubes, all that rich and subtle biological orography that lay beneath the smooth epidermis of Lucrecia's belly. Exists on the inside or the outside of her, he thought. Because everything about her is—or can be—erogenous.

He was not exaggerating, carried away by the tenderness that her sudden appearance in his fantasies always gave rise to. No, absolutely not. For thanks to his unyielding perseverance, he had managed to fall in love with the whole and with each one of the parts of his wife, to love, separately and together, all the components of that cellular universe. He knew himself capable of responding erotically, with a prompt, robust erection, to the stimulus of any of its infinite ingredients, including the meanest and humblest, including what—to the ordinary hominid—was the most inconceivable and most repellent. "Here lies Don Rigoberto, who contrived to love the epigastrium of his spouse as much as her vulva or her tongue," he philosophically projected as a fitting epitaph on the marble of his tomb. Would that mortuary motto be a lie? Not in the slightest. He thought of how impassioned he would become, very shortly, when the sound of muffled aqueous displacements reached his ears, avidly flattened against her soft stomach, and at this moment he could already hear the lively burbling of that flatus, the joyous cracking of a fart, the gargle and yawn of her vagina, or the languid stretching of her serpentine intestine. And he could already hear himself whispering, blind with love and lust, the phrases with which it was his habit to render his wife homage as he caressed her. "Those little noises, too, are you, Lucrecia; they are your characteristic harmony, your resounding person." He was certain that he would not have the opportunity to verify, since he would never embark upon the experiment of hearing love with any other woman. Wasn't Lucrecia an ocean of unfathomable depths that he, the lover-diver, would never have done with exploring? "I love you," he murmured, feeling once again the dawn of an erection.

—TRANSLATED BY HELEN LANE

on "LOVE'S FIRST APPROACH"

Tell me, lovers, when do you know? A lot of "Love at first ____" phrases get volleyed about: first sight, first kiss, first touch (the jaded among us might add first fuck, frig or fellation, not to forget *Love at First Bite*—that celluloid George Hamilton vehicle, mainstay of my family's communal video-viewing pleasure). But when do you know that you have moved from hoping to having, from a future indeterminate to a future determinate, from a life lived in one to a life lived in two? Is there a moment when you feel that you have just, that second, fallen in love, as when you touch your forehead and say, "That was a raindrop"? Or is it like the flick of a razor, so subtle and sharp there is no pain, not even recognition? One day you find a photo framed on your desk, a message on your machine from someone else's mother, a ring tucked deep in your pocket. Maybe you deliberate on using the word, holding it back till you're absolutely sure, or maybe it just slips out one day, and there it is. In almost all things of consequence—history, philosophy, human emotions—the materiality of change lags behind the reality of the having been changed. The rational mind, looking for evidence, is never able to account for the gap. There are only phrases like: "You wake up one morning . . . " By the time you know you know, the truth has probably long been staring you in the face, watching your movements, wondering when you would finally wake to it. Not so for the pseudonymous seventeenth-century poet Ephelia. In the poem below, she sees and she knows: Strephon is her man. Literature tells us this can happen; life, perhaps, does not. Let us only hope that, however tardily, we come to know (and to feel for what it is) love's rush, flush and feather-heavy crush.

from Ephelia's "LOVE'S FIRST APPROACH"

Strephon I saw, and started at the sight,
And interchangeably look'd red and white;
I felt my blood run swiftly to my heart,
And a chill trembling seize each outward part:
My breath grew short, my pulse did quicker beat,
My heart did heave, as it would change its seat:
A faint cold sweat o'er all my body spread,
A giddy megrim wheel'd about my head:
When for the reason of this change I sought,
I found my eyes had all the mischief wrought;
For they my soul to Strephon had betray'd,
And my weak heart his willing victim made:
The traitors, conscious of the treason,
They had committed 'gainst my reason,
Look'd down with such bashful guilty fear,
As made their fault to every eye appear.
Though the first fatal look too much had done,
The lawless wanderers would still gaze on,
Kind looks repeat, and glances steal, till they
Had look'd my liberty and heart away:
Great Love, I yield; send no more darts in vain,
I am already fond of my soft chain;
Proud of my fetters, so pleas'd with my state,
That I the very thought of freedom hate.
O mighty Love! They art and power join,
To make his frozen breast as warm as mine;
But if thou try'st and can'st not make him kind,
In love such pleasant, real sweets I find;
That though attended with despair it be,
'Tis better still than a wild liberty.

𝕴 don't recall ever having been caught masturbating, but I'm not sure that means I never have been. I remember in high school stopping one night while biking home from a party so I could jerk off behind some shrubs on the University of Illinois campus, only to wake up the next morning fully dressed but partially revealed behind self-same bushes. In broad daylight with my fly open, in other words— but theoretically, not caught. Another time I woke up in my grand- mother's living room, apparently having sleepwalked from the bedroom wearing nothing but a pair of shoes (laces tied). Again, morn- ing came and I was showing, but I don't think I got busted.

Being caught wanking would seem likely to create either the kind of memory to be burned irremovably into one's consciousness by the arcwelder of shame, or alternately snowed under by thickest repres- sion. Who knows? It's probably a function of when you get busted; by one's teen years, I suspect you'd be unlikely to forget. But before? It's hard to say.

It's another matter entirely, however, to be caught masturbating in your sixties. By your best friend. In his daughter's bedroom. In the tub. Looking at a photo of her—or so Philip Roth would have us believe.

For yes, while most of you will remember the masturbatory hijinks of teenaged Portnoy, it's easy to forget that the much older Roth revisited similar territory with a much older protagonist in his 1995 novel *Sabbath's Theater*. Mickey Sabbath, sixty-some-year-old pup- peteer and pervert, has lost his longtime mistress, Drenka, and goes into a life tailspin, finally ending up on his friend Norman's doorway to ask for help. Norman puts Sabbath up in his daughter Deborah's bed- room, and Sabbath does what any truly depraved inveterate perv would do: ransack the room looking for revealing pictures of the daugh- ter. Taking the best he can find, he then retires to her bathroom for a

wank in the tub, and Norman walks in. What I like about this scene is the near silence of both older men in the face of the obvious; a grotesque breach has taken place, and yet... Both are old enough to know the simple truth: this is life.

from Philip Roth's SABBATH'S THEATER

While Sabbath ran a bath in the girlishly pink-and-white bathroom just off Deborah's room, he interested himself in the contents, all jumbled together, of the two drawers beneath the sink... The one item at all beguiling, aside from the tampons, was a tube of vaginal lubricating cream twisted back on itself and nearly empty. He removed the cap to squeeze a speck of the amber grease into the palm of his hand and rubbed it between his thumb and his middle finger, remembering things as he smeared the stuff over his fingertips, all sorts of things about Drenka. He screwed the cap back on and set the tube out for experimentation later...

Before getting into the bath, he trundled in the nude back to her bedroom and took from the desk the largest picture of her he could find... All Sabbath did for the moment was lie in the wonderful warm bath in the pink-and-white-tiled bathroom and scrutinize the picture, as though in his gaze lay the power to transport Deborah home to her tub. Reaching out with one arm, Sabbath was able to raise the lid to expose the seat of Deborah's pink toilet. He rubbed his hand round and round the satiny seat and was just beginning to harden when there was a light rap on the bathroom door. "You all right in there?" Norman asked and pushed the door open a ways to be sure Sabbath wasn't drowning himself.

"Fine," said Sabbath. It had taken no time to retract his hand from the toilet seat, but the photograph was in the other hand and the twisted tube of vaginal cream was up on the counter. He held out the picture so that Norman could see which one it was. "Deborah," Sabbath said.

"Yes. That is Deborah."

"Sweet," said Sabbath.

"Why do you have the photograph in the bathtub?"

"To look at it." . . .

"It would be a shame," Norman finally said, "If it got wet."

on FALCONER

JOHN CHEEVER

I've never asked another man if he looks. I don't normally, but sometimes I sneak a quick peek. It's hard not to: you're standing there at a porcelain urinal with little to do but hold on and shake. Do you just stare at the tiling, do you yawn and raise a hand to the mouth (suggesting a possible hygienic foul to your co-micturators), do you close your eyes and take a deep yogic breath . . . or do you look, just a little? It's natural; most of us hetero men get few opportunities to see other men's members, and it's a curious lot out there. Seeing a little chickee barely poking its head out of the pubic nest puts a lilt in my step that lasts all day. But witnessing a neighbor's whizzing anaconda—that will depress me for hours. Pissing and looking: it's a dangerous dice roll.

Now, pissing and listening: I've definitely never heard another man talk about that. But we all do it, or at least I do. And sadly, my bladder is about the size of a decorative teacup. Which leads to decidedly short, entirely non-splashy, hardly Niagara-like discharges. It's embarrassing, and I feel like half a man. (Especially in truck stops. Jesus, those guys.) So I make up for it with an ace up my sleeve: when I'm pissing, I have good control, so I tend to lift both arms in the air for an extended stretch. I leave my flanking flooders to conclude what they will about my manhood. It's a dog-eat-dog world, the men's.

But no bathroom scene I've ever read compares to John Cheever's account of the masturbation trough in the prison bathroom called "The Valley." Rows of men lined up, each in full regalia, doing his most privy business. More than any other author, Cheever describes the disparities of that uniquely male appurtenance, and the varieties of technique and crescendo to the simple act of self-love. Though any bathroom experience will tell you that not all men are created equal, only Cheever tells us how unequal we in fact are.

from John Cheever's FALCONER

The Valley was a long room off the tunnel to the left of the mess hall. Along one wall was a cast-iron trough of a urinal ... The Valley was where you went after chow to fuck yourself ... There were ground rules. You could touch the other man's hips and shoulders, but nothing else. The trough accommodated twenty men and twenty men stood there, soft, hard or halfway in either direction, fucking themselves. If you finished and wanted to come again you went to the end of the line. There were the usual jokes. How many times, Charlie? Five coming up, but my feet are getting sore.

Considering the fact that the cock is the most critical link in our chain of survival, the variety of shapes, colors, sizes, characteristics, dispositions and responses found in this rudimentary tool are much greater than those shown by any other organ of the body. They were black, white, red, yellow, lavender, brown, warty, wrinkled, comely and silken, and they seemed, like any crowd of men on a street at closing time, to represent youth, age, victory, disaster, laughter and tears. There were the frenzied and compulsive pumpers, the long-timers who caressed themselves for half an hour, there were the groaners and the ones who sighed, and most of the men, when their trigger was pulled and the fusillade began, would shake, buck, catch their breath and make weeping sounds, sounds of grief, of joy, and sometimes death rattles.

on NOTES OF A DIRTY OLD MAN

CHARLES BUKOWSKI

It's an oft-noted double standard: when men have a lot of lovers, they're called studs; when women do, they're called sluts. I've had any number of conversations with male friends about their frustrations with their girlfriends' active pasts. At such times, the fabulous Rodney Dangerfield joke always comes to mind. It goes something like this:

> "So does your wife give good head?"
> "Yeah, fantastic head."
> "You mean she gives halfway decent head?"
> "Yeah, she's absolutely amazing."
> "You mean she kinda knows what she's doing in that department?"
> "Yeah, she's simply marvelous."
> "So how do you think she got so good . . . ?"

While it's pretty clear that there's a logical rift in men wanting women to be virginal and then lamenting when they don't put out, the more subtle contradiction that Dangerfield is on to, of course, is that practice makes more perfect, and more tends to make for merrier. This is an important reminder for those men who would criticize some women for being promiscuous and others for having bum bedroom technique. I, personally, would have all my lovers be old pros. I want them to have enough sexual acumen that they realize sex isn't just skill; I want them in permanent communion with their skin and response; I want them to have the laid-back confidence that old jazz musicians have, and I want us to be able to improvise, to roll with each other's changes, to work in each other's beat, jive with the melody, stay in key. Sex is a kind of extemporized duet, and I want a jam session.

The excerpt below is from the great raving sex maniac Charles Bukowski, who seems to agree with the perspective I've put forth. He is on a blind date with a fan who's been admiring his work—only trouble is, it's a date to get married. But she says she's a nympho, and when they're married she proves it, thus justifying what lesser fans of promiscuity might have called rashness.

from Charles Bukowski's NOTES OF A DIRTY OLD MAN

I don't know if it was those Chinese snails with the little round ass-holes or if it was the Turk with the purple stickpin or if it was simply that I had to go to bed with her seven or eight or nine or eleven times a week, or something else and something else, and something, but I was once married to a woman, a girl, who was coming into a million dollars, all somebody had to do was die, but there isn't any smog in that part of Texas and they eat well and go to the doctor for a scratch or a sneeze. She was a nympho, there was something wrong with her neck, and to get it down close and fast, it was my poems, she thought my poems were the greatest thing since Black, no mean Blake— Blake. And some of them are. Or something else. She kept writing. I didn't know she had a million. I'm just sitting in a room on N. Kingsley Dr., out of the hospital with hemorrhages, stomach and ass, my blood all over the county general hospital, and they telling me after nine pints of blood and nine pints of glucose, "one more drink and you're dead." This is no way to talk to a suicide head. I sat in that room every night surrounded by full and empty beer cans, writing poems, smoking cheap cigars, very white and weak, waiting for the final wall to fall...

Well, she came out on a bus, mama didn't know, papa didn't know, grandpa didn't know, they were on vacation somewhere and she only had a little change. I met her at the bus station, that is, I sat there drunk waiting for a woman I had never seen to get off a bus, waiting for a woman I had never spoken to, to marry. I was insane. I didn't belong on the streets. The call came. It was her bus. I watched the people swing through the door. And here comes this cute sexy blonde in high heels, all ass and bounce and young, young, twenty-three, and the neck wasn't bad at all. Could that be the one? Maybe she'd missed her bus? I walked up.

"Are you Barbara?" I asked.

"Yes," she said, "I guess you're Bukowski?"

"I guess I am. Should we go?"

"Alright."

We got into the old car and drove to my place.

"I almost got off the bus and went back."

"I don't blame you."

We got on in and I drank some more but she said she wouldn't go to bed with me until we got married. So we got some sleep and I drove all the way to Vegas and back. We were married. I drove all the way to Vegas and back without rest, and then we got into bed and it was worth it. The first time. She had told me she was a nymph but I hadn't believed it. After the third or fourth round I began to believe it. I knew that I was in trouble. Every man believes that he can tame a nymph but it only leads to the grave—for the man...

The crazy people up front who had once lived there had put these shelves all around the bed and on these shelves were pots and pots of geraniums. Big pots, little pots. All geraniums. When we fucked the bed would shake the walls and the walls would shake the shelves, and then I'd hear it: the slow volcano sound of the shelves giving away and then I'd stop. "No, no, don't stop, oh Jesus, don't stop!" and I'd catch the stroke again and down those shelves would come, down on my back and ass and head and legs and arms, and she'd laugh and scream and make it. She loved those pots. "I'm gonna rip those shelves off the wall," I would tell her. "Oh, no," she'd say. "Oh please, please don't!" She said it so nicely that I couldn't. So I'd hammer the shelves back, put the pots back on and we'd wait for the next time.

_on_ "THE KISSES"

JOHANNES SECUNDUS

T hirty-two years I've been alive, half of them spent looking for love. My reading this week has brought me to a new clarity, a honing in on what I'm really after. As it turns out, I think I'm only asking for one thing; perhaps it's not too much. Love as delicacy, the gentleness of one who knows, who loves you not like flame raging through newsprint, nor like an axe, butt end or blade, but as the tap of sea ripples against the side of a wooden hull: a steady sound we hear around us, bumping, sustaining, syncopating—beneath, against and everywhere.

I am older now, and I'd like to think I have learned enough to trade passion for permanence, ravagement for rest. There have been times when I've asked love with its hot hand to take me away from life, to consume and devour, to rid me of all senses save the sense of heat itself; now I ask love not to replace being but just to be, to take over, to be the air breathed in and out, so that we are always, invariably, aswim.

It is quieter, this kind of love; we all know that. It seems less sexy, perhaps, till you know it, till you feel that sexy can be the snag and tangle of _here_ unskeined by the nimble fingers of _now_. Your hands, darling, on my brow: that is all I ask.

And so, delicacy itself: a love poem by Johannes Secundus...

Johannes Secundus's **"THE KISSES"**

Kiss XIII

O my dear, my life-languid and spent from our sweet struggle
    I lie,
And breathlessly let my fingers stray about your neck,
My mouth is dry and burning; no air comes
To renew the life of my ravaged heart.

In this state, I saw Charon approaching in his little skiff
Felt the waves of Styx lapping near, too near
Till you came with a kiss, wet on my mouth,
To return me sweetly from the banks of Hell . . .

So, come, Darling, join your lips to mine,
Let my soul be nourished by yours, mouth on mouth,
Until later, when our passion has run its full course,
And a single stream of life from our two bodies has flowed.

on INSTRUCTIONS FOR UNDRESSING
THE HUMAN RACE

FERNANDO ALEGRIA

Many years ago, in a used bookstore in Providence, I came across a tiny little volume of poetry called *Instructions for Undressing the Human Race*. I was intrigued by the title, of course, but I had never heard of the poet, Fernando Alegria, nor had I become the miner of naughty bits that I am today. But one element ensured that I would buy the weird little tome: it was illustrated by Matta, the Chilean painter whose canvas *X Space and the Ego* arrested me the first time I saw it in the Museum of Modern Art, and so terrified and entranced me that I stood looking at it for over half an hour.

Flipping through the pages of *Undressing*, I was similarly disturbed. The drawings were true to the Matta I had seen before: bodies made of disengaged genitalia and weaponry fuckmurdering each other, a chaos of limbs, enigmatic figures and other surreal, scary images— perhaps altogether too much like the id on parade. Alegria's poems that accompanied them were not dissimilar. They suggested removing policemen's boots with the feet still in them and burning firemen in their own flames; there were instructions for undressing your best friend's wife (quickly!); for denuding archangels and the Earth, the artist, the Statue of Liberty, the dictator and Death. Not every poem was so gruesome—some, including the ones I've highlighted here, had an abiding lyricism—but overall I had never read anything that was supposed to be sexy and yet was so irremediably violent. The book scared me, and I put it on my uppermost shelf, out of reach.

Now, more than a decade later, I've taken it down again, hoping it will shed light on the vexing question of the unrepressed libido. What does desire desire? What are the contours of the id? If you have occasion to visit New York, go to MoMA and see Matta's take; for the time being, however, read these poems by Alegria and see if they help lift the superego's skirts.

from Fernando Alegria's
INSTRUCTIONS FOR
UNDRESSING THE HUMAN RACE

IV.
Undress the nun wholly
But respect that white-winged coif during her moon-flight
And the celestial habit will fall away slowly
And the body shoot out like a trembling finger
Sad and feverish.
Wait for her on your knees
Then she will be a capsized goblet bleeding on the beach.

XV.
Undress the Buddhist monk of his flames
Cover him with a red parasol
Anoint his dark face with oil
Perfume his thighs with the breath of a maiden
Wrap his body in silk neckties
Break open pomegranates on his lips
Squeeze a dove on top of his head
Don't perturb him; love him from afar
Allow him to flare up
Like a match between the fingers of God.

—TRANSLATED BY MATTHEW ZION
AND LENNART BRUCE

What is sought with difficulty is discovered with more pleasure.
—Saint Augustine, *On Christian Doctrine*

𝕴n the above quote, Augustine is talking about the pleasures of detangling dense Bible verses, but the same might be said of life as a whole. We sapiens like to be tantalized, necks craned, shaking with thirst, as long as we eventually get to drink. Which brings us, as ever, to the subject of love. For while I have known the joy of deferred pleasure (after seemingly interminable games of pursuit and perseverance), I am also a big fan of the matchlight encounter, of instant chemistry—no games, no waiting, no brakes. Give me the here and now, baby, and later on, at the moment you thought you might wait for, just give it to me again.

Sound philosophy, no? The only problem is, the more desire gets realized, the less literature gets produced. For one of the great motives for the spilling of ink is to try to get one's beloved to give it up (don't think I haven't tried it). From the Wife of Bath's "Prologue" (forerunner to Bessie Smith's "Do Your Duty"), to Shakespeare's famous procreation sonnets, to Marvell's "To His Coy Mistress," to the Earl of Rochester's racy entreaties, the history of naughty bits has been in large part a history of frustration. The fulfilled lover is too busy basking to write, right? So it's up to the hankering hack to get anything actually accomplished.

And thank goodness they do, for often the sexiest of scribbles come from the least sexed of authors. Take the short lyric below, line for line probably one of the smokingest things you'll ever read. Written in Greek in the late sixth century (when Christianity had all but stamped out such literature), it's a moving chronicle of an emphatic *No*. But read aloud to the right person, it just might help get you to *Yes*.

Paulus Silentiarius's "TANTALOS"

Mouth to mouth joined we lie, her naked breasts
Curved to my fingers, my fury grazing deep
On the silver plain of her throat,
And then: no more.
She denies me her bed. Half of her body to Love
She has given, half to Prudence.
I die between.

on THE CORRECTIONS   JONATHAN FRANZEN

𝕴n the hierarchy of the senses, smell is the low man on the totem
pole. Human beings have evolved to a point where smell is no
longer necessary for security or survival; these days, most of the
sniffing we do we could just as easily do without (especially, I'll testify,
living in downtown Manhattan). Granted, it's nice to get a whiff of
Chanel #5 when tucking your lips behind Christy Turlington's ear, or getting a downdraft of daisies on a summer stroll, but smell is dispensable,
an empirical afterthought, the baby toe on the foot of sensory input.

However unnecessary smell may be, however, it is not without its
significance in the erotic realm. There, whether we believe in the ani-
malistic power of pheromones or not, it's still pretty clear that our
noses are doing a lot of work in determining who our potential mates
will be, and whether we want to keep them around after they've fulfilled their biological imperative. Perhaps we aren't entirely conscious
of exactly how our lover smells—but their smell is nonetheless part and
parcel of how we come to understand them. I remember dating a
woman in college named Mickey; once, years later, in a different university in a different city I entered a classroom and immediately thought to
myself, *Mickey was here. Right here.* I didn't find her, and perhaps it
wasn't even her, but whoever bore that scent certainly would have gotten an invite from me to go get a beer.

Clearly, of all the senses, smell still has the most currency in its
relation, almost uncanny, to memory. Because it's so hard to pinpoint
smells, we are never as sure as we might be that we know what we've
experienced, nose-wise. Thus when we are reminded of a smell that we
didn't know we knew in the first place, it seems amazing, miraculous,
hard to be believed. But memory, like consciousness itself, is deep,
murky and fast-flowing, and scents are perhaps the strongest dragnet
through its dark depths. Nothing has a stronger déjà-effect than smell,

nothing transports us back so fast. And so in the excerpt below, one of Jonathan Franzen's quirky characters from his National Book Award–winning *The Corrections* seeks to retrieve some vestige of a woman's vagina in the lingering smells on the fibers of a plush chair. Rather compromising, no doubt, but a logical use of the smallest sense in its largest hour.

from Jonathan Franzen's THE CORRECTIONS

The night of Alfred's seventy-fifth birthday had found Chip alone at Tilton Ledge pursuing sexual congress with his red chaise lounge . . .

He was kneeling at the feet of his chaise and sniffing its plush minutely, inch by inch, in hopes that some vaginal tang might still be lingering eight weeks after Melissa Paquette had lain here. Ordinarily distinct and identifiable smells—dust, sweat, urine, the dayroom reek of cigarette smoke, the fugitive afterscent of quim—became abstract and indistinguishable from oversmelling, and so he had to pause again and again to refresh his nostrils. He worked his lips down into the chaise's buttoned navels and kissed the lint and grit and crumbs and hairs that collected in them. None of the three spots where he thought he smelled Melissa was unambiguously tangy, but after exhaustive comparison he was able to settle on the least questionable of the three spots, near a button just south of the backrest, and give it his full nasal attention. He fingered other buttons with both hands, the cool plush chafing his nether parts in a poor approximation of Melissa's skin, until finally he achieved sufficient belief in the smell's reality—sufficient faith that he still possessed some relic of Melissa—to consummate the act. Then he rolled off his compliant antique and slumped on the floor with his pants undone and his head on the cushion, an hour closer to having failed to call his father on his birthday.

A lover or a fighter? I suspect there's a reason the Lord gave me a good flight impulse. Though I lean strongly (and willfully) to Cupid's side of the question, I still find it a curious dichotomy. Why must we pick just one? And why, when saying one's a lover not a fighter, do people normally sound a bit apologetic, like being a lover is the booby prize you get for not being the town bully?

It could be the lingering cultural impact from the first major work of European literature: Homer's *The Iliad*. Written approximately ten centuries before the birth of Christ, *The Iliad* takes great pains to divide men into the two camps and to generally have the amorous get their asses waxed by the bellicose. At times, the degree to which beauty and facility in love are punished in *The Iliad* seems almost comical; at one point, even the love goddess Aphrodite gets slapped around by war goddess Athena. But nowhere does one see the antagonism expressed as clearly as in the fight between Menelaus and Paris over Helen, the woman they both want, whose abduction sets the whole war in motion.

To recap: Paris and the Trojans paid a visit to the Greek Achaians and went back to Troy with the Greek prince Menelaus's wife, Helen. Wife-nabbing apparently didn't go over so well back then, so Menelaus and his brother Agamemnon assemble a couple hundred warships and sail to the Trojan coast to sack the city and get Helen back. Ten years later, the groups are still fighting with no end in sight, so Menelaus and Paris agree to fight one-on-one to see who wins the mega-hottie.

The two men could hardly be more different. Menelaus is constantly described as warlike, tough and broad-chested (if short). Paris, meanwhile, is noted for his full lips, his facial beauty, his way with women and his curly golden locks. Wanna guess who has the upper hand? Before they fight, Hector, Paris's brother, makes clear what's at stake: "Evil Paris, beautiful, woman-crazy, cajoling ... [thus will] you learn of the man whose blossoming wife you have taken. The lyre would not help you then, nor the favors of Aphrodite, nor your locks, when you rolled in the dust, nor all your beauty." Ouch. And from his own brother!

So, of course, the fight ensues. Paris is getting mangled and is only saved by intervention of the gods. But here is where it gets interesting: having been delivered back to his castle in a cloud of mist, Paris finds Helen, who proceeds to berate him for having lost the battle. His response sets up the naughty bit below. And, indeed, if one can't truly be both a lover and a fighter, make no mistake as to which is preferable. Take Paris's lead and embrace the shame, while you're embracing everything else.

from Homer's THE ILIAD

Pray thee, woman, cease to chide and grieve me thus.
Disgraces will not ever last: look on their end—on us
Will other Gods, at other times, let fall the victor's wreath,
As on Menelaus Pallas puts it now. Shall our love sink beneath
The hate of fortune? In love's fire let all hates vanish. Yes, to
      bed,
Then, let us go, and turn ourselves to love-making instead,
Come, love has never so inflamed these senses of mine
Not when I took you from Lakedaimon the first time,
And caught you, and with you on a bed of love did lay
Along the shore of the lovely island of Kranae.
With this they moved to the odorous bed,
And there on pleasure and love's delight they fed,
While Menelaus, savage-like, did stamp and search the field
For his mortal foe who would not yield . . .

—ADAPTED FROM THE GEORGE CHAPMAN
TRANSLATION BY JACK MURNIGHAN

on POEMS AND BALLADS
A. C. SWINBURNE

𝕬h, the hickey. Such a marker, such a brand, more symbolic and defiant even than a tattoo. A hickey says, *I've been messing around and I'm not afraid to show it, not to mention that I'm also rather crass and probably in deep economic hardship and I'm not afraid to show that either.* Being where I'm from, the corn country of Illinois, hickeys were a pretty big part of the social economy of my high school. I remember proud Camaro-drivers in the locker room describing to us, their captive audience of weenies, the necklace of hickeys they had left on their loved ones the night before in the church parking lot. I remember seeing enormous, purplebrownorangecrimson splotches like phantasmagoric blood-sucking sea flowers grafted onto the necks of my PE mates. I heard tales of initials being spelled on asses, of hearts crudely sketched, of yellow- and brick-colored roads leading from clavicle to cunny, left by the champing lips of rear-seat Romeos. And I thought, *This is romance.*

I would not receive my first hickey till senior year—and it proved to be a force of history. But, as Marx reminds us, history is as much farce as it is tragedy, and this tale has equal dollops of both. It was a summer evening, one of my friend's parents were away, the party was raging and I snuck out the back with someone else's girlfriend. We were lying in the wet grass making out and I thought, *This is the most beautiful woman I will ever kiss.* And then came the voice of her boyfriend. She jumped up and went back while I slinked into the night. The next day, I was supposed to meet friends at the pool. I woke to find a half-dollar-sized mottled bruise just below my right ear. Impossible to hide. I arrived at the pool to find not only my friends, but a different young woman whom I had been courting forever, the one I really wanted, Junior Miss Right, ready to set her towel down next to mine. And then she saw it. There was no *not* seeing it, and I knew it. I sheepishly tried to explain, but she didn't say anything. She just turned, as little tears started to form in her eyes, and went back to the changing rooms. There was never another chance.

But, marked as my life has been by hickeys, I never really noticed them coming up in literature. Not, that is, until Swinburne. Based on the frequency of references, it would appear that old A. C. was not capable of kissing without marking, of osculating without masticating. Here are a few examples I found in Swinburne's most important book of poetry, *Poems and Ballads*. This may not be a comprehensive list, but I think it's more than enough to crown Swinburne "Poet of the Hickey."

from A. C. Swinburne's POEMS AND BALLADS

from "Laus Veneris"
Asleep or waking is it? For her neck,
Kissed over close, wears yet a purple speck
Wherein the pained blood falters and goes out;
Soft, and stung softly—fairer for a fleck.
[...]
There is a feverish famine in my veins;
Below her bosom, where a crushed grape stains
The white and blue, there my lips caught and clove
An hour since, and what mark of me remains?
[...]
Alas! For sorrow is all the end of this.
O sad kissed mouth, how sorrowful it is!
O breast whereat some suckling sorrow clings,
Red with the bitter blossom of a kiss!

from "Fragoletta"
Mine arms are close about thine head,
My lips are fervent on thy face,
And where my kiss hath fed

Thy flower-like blood leaps red
To the kissed place.

from "Dolores: Notre Dame des Sept Douleurs"
By the ravenous teeth that have smitten
Through the kisses that blossom and bud
[...]
The white wealth of a body made brighter
By the blushes of amorous blows,
And seamed with sharp lips and fierce fingers,
And branded by kisses that bruise
[...]
The skin changes country and color
And shrivels or swells to a snake's
Let it brighten and bloat and grow duller,
We know it, the flames and the flakes,
Red brands on it smitten and bitten,
Round skies where a star is a stain,
And the leaves with thy litanies written,
Our Lady of Pain.

The great works are dying. Dying, not because they are losing their relevance in our age of machine and microchip, nor because they are languishing in the dustiest corners of soon-to-be-obsolete libraries, nor even because recession and pragmatism are turning the universities more and more into trade schools (perhaps rightly); they are dying because we are losing the languages in which they were written, and translation is no more than a stopgap. My own linguistic limitations are indicative: though I'm conspicuously over-trained as a pedant, I still cannot read Greek, nor do any of my friends. I have to get my Plato in translation, and I can never trust my own instincts on the cryptic but beautiful fragments of Anaximander or Parmenides. The sublimity of Sophocles and Aeschylus will always be secondhand for me, and Homer—the bridge of gods and men—will always sound a bit forced and tinny in my ear. For centuries, the intel-lectual elite of Europe believed that ancient Greece was the pinnacle of human civilization, yet I, and most everyone else in today's version of civilized life, will never be able to appreciate the full force of why.

Sad as I am about the loss of so many great writers, I am perhaps most saddened by not being able to read in the original the foremost romantic and lyric poet of antiquity, Sappho. Most people know Sappho only for her lesbianism (a term which derives from Sappho having run a school for girls on the isle of Lesbos), but for centuries she was regarded as among history's greatest poets. As recently as a hundred years ago, English schoolboys were assigned Sappho in Greek as part of their clas-sics homework, despite the strong sexual overtones of many of her poems. Nowadays, even if high school students were capable of reading the language, Sappho would never make it past school board censors. And it's a shame. Her poems, which exist mostly in fragments, exhibit an emotional depth and delicacy (even in translation) that no writer would match for a thousand years. Take the selection below, "Anactoria," perhaps Sappho's most famous poem, which describes the psychosomatic effects that love has on a person. It reads like a highly poeticized list of side effects to some heavy-duty medicine: dry mouth, chest pains, wandering thoughts—you get the picture. It's been 2,600 years since Sappho wrote this poem to one of her students, and I'm not sure anyone has done a better job describing the physical herk and jerk of a massive crush.

Note: As I can't fully endorse any one English translation of Sappho's works, I read renderings of "Anactoria" in all the languages I know, then tried to improve on the best I could find. The result, I hope, captures a bit of the quiddity of the original. But then—if one takes the hardest line on such matters—how would I (or almost anyone else) really know? Not, at least, till we spend more time in the language lab...

Sappho's "ANACTORIA"

He who sits in your presence,
Listening close to your sweet speech and laughter,
Is, in my esteem, yet luckier than the gods.
The thought makes my heart aflutter in my breast.
For even seeing you but briefly,
I lose what words I had;
My tongue finds not a sound;
My eyes fail to see, my ears set to ring;
A fire runs beneath my skin;
Sweat pours from me and a trembling takes my body whole.
I am paler than summer-burned grass, and, in my madness
I fear that I too may die.
And yet, I'll dare it. Just a little more!

—ADAPTED BY JACK MURNIGHAN
FROM THE HENRY WHARTON TRANSLATION

he tables are soon to turn: for the first twenty-seven years of my life, I was the elder of two brothers, but five years ago my father remarried and I now have two sisters as well—one step, one half, the eldest about to go to high school. What does this mean? It means that I'm changing from a guy who spent his life trying to seduce other guys' sisters to one trying to protect his own. I can't believe it's happening; all those years of mocking my friends for various attempts to put their fairer siblings off-limits, and now it's my turn. The gods of irony (the only ones there are) are chortling from the ether.

The worst part is, I know from both literature and experience that all my prohibitory efforts are only likely to encourage both sisters and suitors. Haven't people realized yet, isn't everyone fully aware by now, that prohibition creates enticement? Too easily I think back on Juliet sneaking out the back window, or of Heloise tricking her five brothers so she could be with her lover, Abelard. (Though I should point out to my sisters' future would-be's that the brothers did catch up to Abelard and castrate him.) I remember when sisters would visit my male friends in college and I'd be told, with minimal ambiguity, "on pain of death"— only to find myself making her coffee in the morning. Such is the way of the world. Sisters tend to like their brothers; brothers tend to like their friends; the transitive property would suggest, then, that sisters tend to like their brothers' friends (and the reverse is certainly true). Go ahead, try and stop mathematical law.

It works in my favor, I suppose, that most of my friends are at least twenty years older than my eighth-grade sister. And so, as she crosses the line into her almost-woman self, she is unlikely to be beguiled by their sag and gray. But the rest of maledom! What am I to do? I know how bad they are; I'm one of them! I know too that more than protection from me, what she really needs is support—needs to know that, when mistakes are inevitably made, at least they were her mistakes . . . and that she knows where she can go to talk about it. This, my friends, is what I am going to try to do, but, munificent as I may be, all you lechers are still forewarned.

This excerpt is a case study in brother/sister/friend dynamics. It comes from the unstoppable Henry Miller, who died in 1980, and thus, I am most pleased to say, will never be able to meet my lithe siblings.

from Henry Miller's TROPIC OF CAPRICORN

I can visualize best my condition when I think of my relations with Maxie and his sister Rita. At the time Maxie and I used to go swimming together a great deal, that I remember well. Often we passed the whole day and night at the beach. I had only met Maxie's sister once or twice; whenever I brought up her name Maxie would rather frantically begin to talk about something else. That annoyed me because I was really bored to death with Maxie's company, tolerating him only because he loaned me money readily and bought me things which I needed. Every time we started for the beach I was in hopes his sister would turn up unexpectedly. But no, he always managed to keep her out of reach. Well, one day as we were undressing in the bathhouse and he was showing me what a fine tight scrotum he had, I said to him right out of the blue—"Listen, Maxie, that's all right about your nuts, they're fine and dandy, and there's nothing to worry about, but where the hell is Rita all the time, why don't you bring her along some time and let me take a good look at her quim, yes, quim, you know what I mean." Maxie, being a Jew from Odessa, had never heard the word quim before. He was deeply shocked by my words and yet at the same time intrigued by this new word. In a sort of daze he said to me—"Jesus, Henry, you oughtn't to say a thing like that to me!"

"Why not?" I answered. "She's got a cunt, your sister, hasn't she?" I was about to add something else when he broke into a terrific fit of laughter. That saved the situation, for the time being. But Maxie didn't like the idea at all deep down. All day long it bothered him, though he never referred to our conversation again. No, he was very silent that day. The only form of revenge he could think of was to urge me to swim far beyond the safety zone in the hope of tiring me out and letting me drown. I could see so clearly what was in his mind that I was possessed with the strength of ten men. Damned if I would go drown myself just because his sister like all other women happened to have a cunt . . .

[A few hours later] I thought of Rita, her private and extraordinary quim. I was in the train, bound for New York and dozing off with a marvelous languid erection. And stranger still, when I got out of the train, when I had walked but a block or two from the station, whom should I bump into rounding a corner but Rita herself. And as though she had been informed telepathically of what was going on in my brain, Rita too was hot under the whiskers. Soon we were sitting in a chop suey joint, seated side by side in a little booth, behaving exactly like a pair of rabbits in rut. On the dance floor we hardly moved. We were wedged in tightly and we stayed that way, letting them jog and jostle us about as they might. I could have taken her home to my place, as I was alone at the time, but no, I had a notion to bring her back to her own home, stand her up in the vestibule and give her a fuck right under Maxie's nose—which I did. In the midst of it I thought again of . . . the word quim. I was on the point of laughing aloud when suddenly I felt she was coming, one of those long drawn out orgasms such as you get now and then in a Jewish cunt. I had my hands under her buttocks, the tips of my fingers just inside her cunt, in the lining, as it were; as she began to shudder I lifted her from the ground and raised her gently up and down on the end of my cock. I thought she would go off her nut completely, the way she began to carry on. She must have had four or five orgasms like that in the air, before I put her feet down on the ground. I took it out without spilling a drop and made her lie down in the vestibule. Her hat had rolled off into a corner and her handbag had spilled open and a few coins had tumbled. I note this because just before I gave it to her good and proper I made a mental note to pocket a few coins for my carfare home. Anyway, it was only a few hours since I had said to Maxie in the bathhouse that I would like to take a look at his sister's quim, and here it was now smack up against me, sopping wet and throwing out one squirt after another. If she had been fucked before she had never been fucked properly, that's a cinch. And I myself was never in such a fine cool collected scientific frame of mind as now lying on the floor of the vestibule right under Maxie's nose, pumping it into the private, sacred and extraordinary quim of his sister Rita.

I pose this as an open question: What constitutes sexual addiction? Is it like drinking, where four or five a day signals a problem? Is it like heroin, where you have to do it at any cost? Or like cigarettes, where going without for a whole plane ride is a problem? I ask because I don't know, and I occasionally fear that the propulsion of enthusiasm might cross the line into obsession. Sex is a glorious thing to dedicate much of your life to, and yet, there is a point where sex stops being about sex, where the meaning and experience of the act is replaced by the compulsion of doing. This, I would say, is the point of addiction.

Now, in any discussion of sex addiction it is important to make a distinction between sex and what one might term *seduction addiction*. Sex addiction is a calculus of numbers, not of people. Sex addiction leads to anonymous encounters, to porn, to prostitutes, to whatever is capable of releasing the juice—and the vehicle is irrelevant. Seduction addiction is a different thing: it's about affirmation, about being liked, about being able to persuade. It's about power. If I am in fact concerned about the history of my libidinal behavior, it just might be that seduction addiction is what scares me the most.

But who doesn't want to be liked? It's a rare person who can ignore the opinions of others, and who doesn't seek to reinforce the ego by pleasing. And yet the seduction addict takes this logical, human impulse to a somewhat absurd extreme. There have been times in my life when I needed the constant ego massage of a steady stream of new lovers. Their appeal was not novelty (the usual explanation), nor even variety. It was safety. Safety in numbers, safety in the accumulation of intimacy that—because it is not centered in a single person—seems less precarious, less at the mercy of one beating heart.

Seduction addiction creates an illusion of intimacy that seems safe—this is its appeal. Lucretius, in the first century B.C., advocates

promiscuity as an antidote to the stinging barbs of love. Perhaps, he indicates, one can distract oneself from the true source of pain. I suspect seduction addiction is very much about distraction, trying to forget the loneliness that motivates the frenzy of the quest itself. We hunger, we gaze upon the pastries and hunger all the more. The snake consumes its tail.

from Lucretius's THE NATURE OF THE UNIVERSE

The thing in us that responds to the stimulus is the seed that comes with ripening years and strengthening limbs. For different things respond to different stimuli or provocations. The one stimulus that evokes human seed from the human body is a human form. As soon as this seed is dislodged from its resting-place, it travels through every member of the body, concentrating at certain reservoirs in the loins and promptly acts upon the generative organs. These organs are stimulated and swollen by the seed. Hence follows the will to eject it in the direction in which tyrannical lust is tugging. The body makes for the source from which the mind is pierced by love. For the wounded normally fall in the direction of their wound: the blood spurts out toward the source of the blow; and the enemy who delivered it, if he is fighting at close quarters, is bespattered by the crimson stream. So, when a man is pierced by the shafts of Venus, whether they are launched by a lad with womanish limbs or a woman radiating love from her whole body, he strives toward the source of the wound and craves to be united with it and to transmit something of his own substance from body to body. His speechless yearning is a presentiment of bliss.

    This, then, is what we term Venus. This is the origin of the thing called love — the drop of Venus' honey that first drips into our heart, to be followed by a numbing heartache. Though the object of your love may be absent, images of it will haunt you and the beloved name chimes sweetly in your ears. If you find yourself thus passionately enamored of an individual, you should keep well away from such images. Thrust from you anything that might feed your passion, and turn your mind elsewhere. Vent the seed of love upon other objects. By clinging to it you assure yourself the certainty of heartsickness and pain. With nourishment the festering sore quickens and strengthens. Day by day, the frenzy heightens and the grief deepens. Your only remedy is to lance the first wound with new incisions; to salve it, while it is still fresh, with promiscuous attachments; to guide the motions of your mind into some other channel...

In love there is the hope that the flame of passion may be quenched by the same body that kindled it. But this runs clean counter to the course of nature. This is the one thing of which the more we have, the more our breast burns with the evil lust of having... In the midst of love, Venus teases lovers with images. They cannot glut their eyes by gazing on the beloved form, however closely. Their hands glean nothing from those dainty limbs in their aimless roving over all the body. Then comes the moment when with limbs entwined they pluck the flower of youth. Their bodies thrill with the presentiment of joy, and it is seed-time in the fields of Venus. Body clings greedily to body; moist lips are pressed on lips and deep breaths are drawn through clenched teeth. But all to no purpose. One can glean nothing from the other, nor enter in and be wholly absorbed, body in body; for sometimes it seems that that is what they are craving and striving to do, so hungrily do they cling together in Venus' fetters, while their limbs are unnerved and liquefied by the intensity of rapture. At length, when the spate of lust is spent, there comes a slight intermission in the raging fever. But not for long. Soon the same frenzy returns. The fit is upon them once more. They ask themselves what it is they are craving for, but find no device that will master their malady. In aimless bewilderment they waste away, stricken by an unseen wound.

—TRANSLATED BY RONALD LATHAM

on DANGEROUS LIAISONS Choderlos de Laclos

ost of us have seen a film adaptation of *Dangerous Liaisons*, either Steven Frears's fantastically compelling version of the same name, or Milos Forman's rather less gripping *Valmont*, or perhaps the recent teeny-bopper adaptation starring that young woman who plays Buffy, about which, however, I do not have nor will ever have any further information. Having but seen John Malkovich sneer or Glenn Close rend her makeup, you know what it means to have a great work of literature convert beautifully to the screen. The story, of course, is of two masters of seduction, Valmont and the Marquise de Merteuil, and their attempts to outdo each other with more and more daring, difficult gettings-to-yes. It is literature's foremost document of seduction addiction, and a prolonged study of the seducer's mind. Or, better said, minds, for we eventually discover in both book and film that the motives that drive Valmont and Merteuil's respective exploits differ dramatically. I don't want to give the end away, but I can say that, of the two, only Valmont is the true seduction addict. Certain elements of his character make it clear that at some point sex for him moved from being an emotional to an entirely symbolic thing; this, to me, signals the point of addiction.

I would say that for all of us, sex, like most things in life, contains some measure of both the emotional and the symbolic, and that the challenge is to shift the emphasis from the latter to the former. As a man—or a boy, rather—much of the joy of your first sexual experiences is of just having had it, of notching the belt, of running the bases and doing the various things you'd heard other boys bragging about. I suspect that, for a lot of men, the emotional side of sex continues to take a backseat to its symbolic import. In a certain sense, this could be why husbands are so notorious for losing interest in sex: for them, the act has lost its symbolic element, and they never learned to access any deeper meaning. Sex for them had always been about numbers, and when the counting stops, it loses its allure. This is certainly not true of all men all the time, but I fear it affects us more than we would like to admit.

In Valmont's case, his lifelong shenanigans have left him interested only in belt-notching, and the degree of difficulty is his sole index of pleasure. In the excerpt below, he recounts to Merteuil his first encounters with their young pawn Cecile (the Uma Thurman character in the Frears version), whose staggering physical charms are almost entirely lost on him (as is the chance for any deeper connection). For Valmont, the joy of their encounter lies only in the machination behind it. Pay special attention to the excerpt's last line, and you will see the fate of a sex addict under a microscope.

from Choderlos de Laclos's DANGEROUS LIAISONS

Considering that I always bear in mind your plans as well as mine, I decided to make the most of the opportunity both to ascertain the true potential of this child, and to hasten her education... The little one is most giddy, and to encourage her happiness I had the idea of narrating, during our *intermezzos*, all the scandalous stories that came into my head. To give them an extra spice, and to make her pay closer attention, I attributed them all to her mama, whom it amused me to ascribe with such vices and follies.

It was not without motive that I opted to proceed as such. It encouraged our timid schoolgirl more than anything else would have, and at the same time inspired her with the profoundest disdain for her mother. I observed long ago that even if it is not always necessary to employ this method in seducing a young girl, it can be indispensable and is often the most effective way of corrupting her—for if she has no respect for her mother, she will have no respect for herself. I would find ample opportunity to test this moral truth, which I find rather useful, on our little schoolgirl...

I have already received her twice, and in this short interval the student has become almost as knowledgeable as the master. Yes, truth be told, I have taught her everything, even down to the minor complaisances! Everything, that is, except for the art of taking precautions...

I spend my free moments...composing a kind of catechism of the debauched for the use of my pupil. I amuse myself by not calling anything except by its technical name, and I am already laughing at the interesting conversation this will create with Gercourt on the first night of their marriage. Nothing is more amusing than her innocence in using what little she already knows of this language! She doesn't imagine there is any other way of saying the same things. The child really is seductive! The contrast between her naïve candor and the effrontery of her language could not, of course, fail to make itself felt, and, I don't know why, it is only the bizarre that gives me pleasure now.

—TRANSLATED BY JACK MURNIGHAN

on THE ANANGA RANGA

KALYANA MALLA

Every lover should know bedroom Morse code. Morse code? You mean that stuff they used to use for telegraphs before telephones and instant messaging? Yes, dear, Morse code. Short, long, short. Remember? This is how you do it if you're a man: while erect and inside, give the penis head a little "flex" (i.e. tense the thing so a little extra blood goes to the head; if you do this while you can see it, you can watch the head swell a bit). Short. Now do it again and draw it out. Long. Short, long, short. Pulses, slow dragging. The head of the penis grows, and, in doing so, presses out and back. Your partner will feel the bump deep inside. And can decode it. To spell "more" for example, it's: Long, long. Pause. Long, long, long. Pause. Short, long, short. Pause. Short.

And "I love you"? Short, short. Pause. Short, long, short, short. Pause. Long, long, long. Pause. Short, short, short, long. Pause. Short. Pause. Long, short, long, long. Pause. Long, long, long. Pause. Short, short, long. Not too tough, right? Especially compared to all the other ways we try to say it...

And a woman, how does she transmit? With the famed vaginal constriction, of course, sacred knowledge of history's most successful courtesans. As everyone who knows the right things knows, there are muscles within the vagina that can contract, ring-like, to give the man's penis a little circumferential squeeze, or to grip what it wants to hold on to, or even, some say, to open a Pepsi bottle. Oh my.

And now it can't be hard to imagine the Morse code I'm speaking about. He bumps, she squeezes. Short, long, long, long. Bump, squeeze, bump. Tell each other what you want. Tell how you feel. Say yes. Write God's name.

This excerpt is taken from the Hindu sex manual, *The Ananga Ranga*, a follow-up to the better-known *Kama Sutra*. The passage concerns the fineries of woman-on-top sex, concluding with Sir Richard Burton's delightful footnote about vaginal constriction—and those who know how and those who don't. His lament, that too few women (especially in the West) are aware of and practice said technique, remains true, over a century after his translation and many centuries after *The Ananga Ranga* told us how.

from Kalyana Malla's THE ANANGA RANGA

Purushayitabandha is the reverse of what men usually practice. In this case, the man lies upon his back, draws his wife upon him and enjoys her. It is especially useful when he, being exhausted, is no longer capable of muscular exertion, and when she is ungratified, being still full of the water of love. The wife must, therefore, place her husband supine upon the bed or carpet, mount upon his person and satisfy her desires...

Whilst thus reversing the natural order in all forms of Purushayita, the wife will draw her breath after the fashion called Sitkara; she will smile gently, and she will show a kind of half shame, making her face so attractive it cannot well be described. After which she will say to her husband, "O my dear. O thou rogue; this day thou hast come under my control, and hast become subjected to me, being totally defeated in the battle of love!" Her husband manipulates her hair according to art, embraces her and kisses her lower lip, whereupon all her members will relax, she will close her eyes and fall into a swoon of joy.

Moreover, at all times of enjoying Purushayita, the wife will remember that without an especial exertion of will on her part, the husband's pleasure will not be perfect. To this end, she must ever strive to close and constrict the Yoni [vagina] until it holds the Linga [penis], as with a finger, opening and shutting at her pleasure, and finally, acting as the hand of the Gopala-girl, who milks the cow. This can be learned only by long practice, and especially by throwing the will into the part affected, even as men endeavor to sharpen their hearing, and their sense of touch. While doing so, she will mentally repeat "Kamadeva! Kamadeva!" in order that a blessing may rest upon the undertaking. And she will be pleased to hear that the art once learned is never lost. Her husband will then value her above all women, nor would he exchange her for the most beautiful Rani [queen] in the three worlds. So lovely and pleasant to man is she who constricts.

—TRANSLATED BY SIR RICHARD BURTON

(SIR RICHARD BURTON'S TRANSLATOR'S NOTE: Amongst some races, the constrictor vagina muscles are abnormally developed. In Abyssinia, for instance, a woman can so exert them as to cause pain to a man, and, when sitting upon his thighs, she can induce the orgasm without moving any other part of her person. Such an artist is called by the Arabs "Kabbazah," literally meaning "a holder," and it is not surprising that the slave dealers pay large sums for her. All women have more or less the power, but they wholly neglect it; indeed, there are many races in Europe which have never even heard of it. To these, the words of wisdom spoken by Kalyana Malla, the poet, should be particularly acceptable.)

T here are the great literary themes you learned about in high school—man versus nature, man versus society, man versus self—and then there is the epic struggle of the excerpt below: man versus hair. Hair is an anarchist, an outlaw, a weed. Like liberal ideas, the more you try to keep it in its place, the more it sneaks through, making a muck of things. My own body is under daily pilatory siege: first the beard, then the nose hair, recently a back hair or two (dear God), and now, a few years into my thirties, earlobe hair. How can this be?

As a man, hair is a source of near-constant vexation: first the teen traumas around wanting pubic and chest hair to prove one's virility, then the slow realization that every new body hair signals one fewer head hair. Hair on men migrates, as the head-to-shoulder ratio seen on any Greek-isle beach would attest, and it's hard not to think that the little buggers are moving to the wrong neighborhood.

On women, of course, hair is a more tangled issue, both personally and politically. To shave or not to shave, and what—these questions trace out party lines, even in this decade. Porn and the mass media seem to suggest that men would have women shave everything south of the pate. I disagree. My ideal? Legs, shaved; pubis, trimmed; underarms, either way.

Nor am I particularly wedded to variations one way or the other, except regarding the pussy. A shaved muff (and how, etymologically, can it still be a muff if it's shaved?) strikes me as an odd, even a sad thing. Somehow, I don't want a pussy to look vulnerable, and I certainly don't want it to look child-like. To me, the hair of genitals means sex, means, "Now. I'm ready." And could this not have been the biological function (for what other reason are we furry down there?), to signal to our primitive progenitors who, if dragged into the shadows of the cave, would propagate the tribe?

My sociobiology might be a little shaky here, I realize, and my aesthetic preference might be in the minority. Apparently, a lot of men really do like the babyface-vagina thing, and a lot of women find it sexy too. I present as evidence a scene from Almudena Grandes's *The Ages of Lulu*, which won an award in Spain for best erotic novel of 1989. It's a pretty sexy book—if you like that kind of thing—especially during Lulu's early encounters with Pablo, the friend of her older brother who becomes her sexual mentor. In their first meeting, Pablo takes the fifteen-year-old Lulu back to his apartment and then preps her in a way he finds suited to her age. Like Buck Mulligan at the beginning of *Ulysses*, he comes "bearing a bowl of lather on which a mirror and a razor lay crossed." I suppose the antidote to innocence lost is innocence faked.

from Almudena Grandes's THE AGES OF LULU

He was standing there, with a tray full of things, watching me move my lips, maybe he'd even heard me, but he didn't say anything. He walked across the room and sat down facing me, his legs crossed like an Indian. I thought he was going to eat my pussy—after all, he owed it to me—but he didn't.

He took off my knickers, pulled me abruptly towards him, making me lean my bottom on the edge of the armchair and opened me up even wider, placing my legs over the arms of the chair...

He took a sponge from the tray, plunged it into a bowl of warm water and started to rub it against a bar of soap, until it was frothy...

I couldn't believe what he was doing. He'd put out his hand and was soaping me with the sponge. He was washing me as if I were a little girl. That threw me completely.

"What are you doing?"

"None of your business."

"It's my cunt, what you do to it is my business." My words sounded ridiculous, and he didn't answer...

He took a razor blade out of his shirt pocket. "What are you going to do with that?"

He gave me his best "don't worry" sort of look, although he kept a firm hold of my thighs, in case I tried anything.

"It's for you," he answered. "I'm going to shave your cunt."

"No way!" I flung myself forward with all my might and tried to get up, but I couldn't. He was much stronger than me.

"Yes." He seemed as calm as ever. "I'm going to shave it and you're going to let me. All you've got to do is keep still. It won't hurt. I've done it loads of times..."

"Why are you doing this?"

"Because you're very dark; you're too hairy for a fifteen-year-old. You don't have a little girl's cunt. And I like little girls' cunts, especially when I'm about to debauch them. Don't worry, just let me get on with it...

"There you are, Lulu, almost done. That wasn't so bad, was it?"

"No, but it really itches."

"I know. It'll itch even more tomorrow, but you look much prettier." He'd leaned back for a moment, to look at his handiwork, I suppose, before disappearing once more between my legs. "Beauty is a monster, a bloodthirsty deity which demands constant sacrifices, as my mother says."

"Your mother's an idiot," I blurted out.

"No doubt she is..."

He kissed me twice, on the inside of my left thigh. Then he put his hand out and took an amber-colored glass jar from the tray, opened it and dipped in his fingers, the index and middle fingers of his right hand.

It was cream. A thick, white, fragrant cream.

His fingers slid over my newly shaved labia, leaving the cream on my skin. I shivered again; it was ice cold... "Aren't you going to rub it in?"

"No, you do it."

I stretched out my hand, wondering what it would feel like... I found it hard to stop. The temptation was too strong, and I let my fingers slide inside, once, twice, over the swollen sticky flesh. Pablo moved closer, inserted his finger very gently, then removed it and put it in my mouth. As I was sucking it, I heard him murmur, "Good girl."

He was kneeling on the floor in front of me. He took me by the waist, pulled me towards him abruptly and made me fall off the armchair.

The shock was brief. He handled me with great ease, in spite of the fact that I was—am—very big.

He made me turn around and kneel, my cheek resting on the seat, my hands barely touching the carpet. I couldn't see him, but I could hear him.

"Stroke yourself till you're about to come, then tell me."

—TRANSLATED BY SONIA SOTO

on "THE ECSTASY"

Having always conceived of these naughty bits as a kind of intellectual smoke-break or literary petit four, I normally try to keep the excerpts bite-sized, toothsome and easy to digest. This bit, however, requires a bit more chewing—but it's well worth it. I have written before on the incomparable verbal complexity of John Donne's poems, how they are like crafty *trompes l'oeil* that appear to be different things depending on how far away you are when you look at them. Donne is like a mad maze-builder, anticipating his reader's movements, leading you down promising paths that quickly dead-end, turning you around, doubling you back, only to show you the secret exit where you least expected it. Apart from Shakespeare, no writer prior to Donne could so deftly construct and extinguish worlds with the break of each poetic line; nor has any writer matched him since.

"The Ecstasy" is a prime example. It begins with an image that one is likely to take for sex: a violet resting its head upon a swollen pillow. But then Donne takes great pains to indicate that it's not sex he's talking about; the violet is his head, the pillow her tummy and they are just sitting still, holding hands, gazing into each other's eyes all day! At which point he begins a lengthy discourse on the great refinement of this kind of non-sexual touching; it is, he contends, the true language that souls speak to one another.

This accounts for the first half of the poem, right up until he mentions the word violet again. The only problem is, beginning with the second mention, the violet is clearly no longer Donne's higher head, but his nether one, getting larger, mingling with the other, and flowing. We are back to the penis, back to sex, which proves to be the still truer language of souls. Sex is the subtle knot that makes us human; soul flows into soul in the act of sex.

But doesn't this contradict the first half of the poem? What about the quiet hand-holding? The truth is, from the Middle Ages forward, the most sophisticated poets would occasionally create poems with two entirely separate and even contradictory meanings; these meanings weren't supposed to invalidate each other, but to coexist simultaneously in the mind of the reader. Not either/or, but both/and. The point of Donne's poem is that there are indeed two violets, two heads, two ways for souls to converse: the quiet, gentle, delicate way your pastor would be proud of, and that other means we normally call humping.

John Donne's "THE ECSTASY"

Where, like a pillow on a bed
A pregnant bank swell'd up to rest
The violet's reclining head,
Sat we two, one another's best.
Our hands were firmly cemented
With a fast balm, which thence did spring;
Our eye-beams twisted, and did thread
Our eyes upon one double string;
So to intergraft our hands, as yet
Was all the means to make us one,
And pictures in our eyes to get
Was all our propagation.
As 'twixt two equal armies fate
Suspends uncertain victory,
Our souls (which to advance their state
Were gone out) hung 'twixt her and me.
And whilst our souls negotiate there,
We like sepulchral statues lay;
All day, the same our postures were,
And we said nothing, all the day.
If any, so by love refin'd

That the soul's language understood,
And by good love were grown all mind,
Within convenient distance stood,
He (though he knew not which soul spake,
Because both meant, both spake the same)
Might thence a new concoction take
And part far purer than he came.
This ecstasy doth unperplex,
We said, and tell us what we love;
We see by this it was not sex,
We see we saw not what did move;
But as all several souls contain
Mixture of things, they know not what,
Love these mix'd souls doth mix again
And makes both one, each this and that.
A single violet transplant,
The strength, the color, and the size,
(All which before was poor and scant)
Redoubles still, and multiplies.
When love with one another so
Interinanimates two souls,
That abler soul, which thence doth flow,
Defects of loneliness controls.
We then, who are this new soul, know
Of what we are compos'd and made,
For th'atomies of which we grow
Are souls whom no change can invade.
But oh alas, so long, so far,
Our bodies why do we forbear?
They are ours, though they are not we; we are
The intelligences, they the spheres.
We owe them thanks, because they thus
Did us, to us, at first convey,
Yielded their senses' force to us,

Nor are dross to us, but allay.
On man heaven's influence works not so,
But that it first imprints the air;
So soul into the soul may flow,
Though it to body first repair.
As our blood labors to beget
Spirits, as like souls as it can,
Because such fingers need to knit
That subtle knot which makes us man,
So must pure lovers' souls descend
T' affections, and to faculties,
Which sense may reach and apprehend,
Else a great prince in prison lies.
To our bodies turn we then, that so
Weak men on love reveal'd may look;
Love's mysteries in souls do grow,
But yet the body is his book.
And if some lover, such as we,
Have heard this dialogue of one,
Let him still mark us, he shall see
Small change, when we are to bodies gone.

on TESS OF THE D'URBERVILLES THOMAS HARDY

𝔍 t goes without saying that English society during the Victorian period is famous for its counter-sexual attitudes. Yet as a culture's machinery of repression becomes more and more powerful, whatever resistance there is to that machinery tends to go underground, and what remains above becomes ever more covert and cryptic. In Victorian erotic writing, the first path was that taken by the anonymous author of *My Secret Life* (an eleven-volume diary of sexual licentiousness); the second path can be seen in Thomas Hardy's classic novel, *Tess of the D'Urbervilles*.

Tess is the gut-rending story of the travails of a peasant girl whose father discovers he is a distant descendent of a prestigious English bloodline. He sends Tess to meet the remaining members of the family, and there begin her misadventures. Hardy's novel does a good job of exposing the backwardness of nineteenth-century English class structure by charting all the individuals who abuse and take advantage of Tess (for though she is inwardly and actually noble, her nobility remains unrecognized, and she ends up harvesting potatoes in frozen fields and dying from abandonment). Yet despite its moral agenda, the novel itself is also willing to exploit Tess. And, predictably, it does so on the sexual front, using the protagonist to create titillation for its otherwise underindulged nineteenth-century readers.

How does this exploitation occur, and how does Hardy make it covert? Not unlike the paintings of the period which, under the guise of high art, present the naked (or suggestively clothed) female form, Hardy writes the scenes building up to the stealing of Tess's virtue in a way that allows the reader to be part of the excitement. While making a superficial moral point about the callousness of nobles and the lack of recourse for raped women, he also mobilizes the dramatic potential of the situation, leaving us with a disquieting feeling of both repulsion and arousal. Scenes like the one below (or paintings like Fragonard's famous *Le Verrou* [The Bolt] in the Louvre), indicate why rape and sexual harassment have always been used as thematic devices: when described, they allow the author to get saucy without compromising his moralistic cover. But perhaps I shouldn't judge Hardy too quickly; I'll let you read the scene below and see if you think he's innocent.

from Thomas Hardy's TESS OF THE D'URBERVILLES

Having mounted beside her, Alec d'Urberville drove rapidly along the crest of the first hill, chatting compliments to Tess as they went...

She began to get uneasy at a certain recklessness in her conductor's driving.

"You will go down slow, sir, I suppose?" she said with attempted unconcern.

D'Urberville looked round upon her, nipped his cigar with the tips of his large white center-teeth, and allowed his lips to smile slowly of themselves.

"Why Tess, isn't it a brave, bouncing girl like you who asks that? Why I always go down at full gallop. There's nothing like it for raising your spirits."

"But perhaps you need not now?"

"Ah," he said, shaking his head, "there are two to be reckoned with. It is not me alone. Tib has to be considered, and she has a very queer temper."

"Who?"

"Why, this mare. I fancy she looked round at me in a very grim way just then. Didn't you notice it?"

"Don't try to frighten me, sir," said Tess stiffly.

"Well, I don't. If any living man can manage this horse, I can. I won't say any living man can do it, but if such has the power, I am he."...

They were just beginning to descend; and it was evident that the horse, whether of her own will or of his (the latter being the more likely), knew so well the reckless performance expected of her that she hardly required a hint from behind.

Down, down they sped, the wheels humming like a top... The wind blew threw Tess' white muslin to her very skin, and her washed hair flew out behind. She was determined to show no open fear, but she clutched d'Urberville's rein-arm.

"Don't touch my arm! We shall be thrown out if you do! Hold on round my waist!"...

She had not considered what she had been doing; whether he were man or woman, stick or stone, in her involuntary hold on him. Recovering her reserve she sat without replying, and thus they reached the summit of another declivity.

"Now then, again!" said d'Urberville.

"No, no!" said Tess. "Show more sense, do, please."...

"Now then, put your arms round my waist again as you did before, my Beauty."

"Never!" said Tess independently, holding on as well as she could without touching him.

"Let me put one little kiss on those holmberry lips, Tess, or even on that warmed cheek, and I'll stop—on my honor, I will!"

Tess, surprised beyond measure, slid farther back still on her seat, at which he urged the horse anew, and rocked her the more.

"Will nothing else do?" she cried at length, in desperation, her large eyes staring at him like those of a wild animal. This dressing her up so prettily by her mother had apparently been to lamentable purpose.

"Nothing, dear Tess," he replied...

"But I don't want anybody to kiss me, sir!" she implored, a big tear beginning to roll down her face, and the corners of her mouth trembling in her attempts not to cry. "And I wouldn't ha' come if I had known!"

He was inexorable, and she sat still, and d'Urberville gave her the kiss of mastery.

Night time / is the right time / to be / with the one you love.

hile I'm sure Ray Charles is an authority on a lot of things, he is not, for obvious reasons, the person most likely to know whether sex is better during the day or at night. I personally have always been of the and/or school of sexuality, but I've known women who only want to have sex under the cloak of darkness, and I once had a male roommate in college who also refused to get nasty *à la lumiere*; I thought him, fittingly, a benighted creature. Sadly, the opinion seems rather widespread that somehow sex in the dark is better than in sunlight, by candlelight, beneath dashboard light, under hot lights or in the narrow beam of a handheld torch. I demur.

In support of my preference, I have heard it said that men are at their best—reproductively speaking—first thing in the morning. The faithful reality of waking wood notwithstanding, this still came as something of a shock to me. Stereotypes would certainly have you believe the reverse: men are famous for getting off, rolling off and commencing to snore; not for starting early so there's more time to cuddle, discuss and repeat after round one is over. No, even if the lab reports are true, evolutionary biology seems to be losing out to the unfortunate work-sleep/work-sleep conditioning of the modern, postindustrial male.

And yet there is still the issue of the morning woody, and erections in general. Many philosophers will tell you that just because the sun rose today doesn't mean it's going to rise tomorrow. It's called the critique of inductive reasoning, and I suspect a lot of men feel the same way about their erections. Frail man, first imperiled by the inexperience of youth, then by the decline of age. Even a decade of successful erections will not erase the memory of one failure, or eliminate the doubt that it could happen again. Which means that somewhere in the back of a man's mind is always the fear that he won't be able to get it up. I believe this accounts, in part, for a lot of men's resistance to sex—for the fact that they are often a lot less interested than their wives or the media would have it. It also accounts for a certain urgency when there is a ready and willing hard-on. It's a poker, clearly, so if it's hot . . .

The poem below is a bit more lighthearted than all that. Attributed to the great Elizabethan explorer and statesman Sir Walter Raleigh, it is a dialogue between a man and woman about when they should get it on. He says now; she says later, when it's dark. Fair jury, I humbly submit: Both?

Sir Walter Raleigh's "DULCINA"

As at noon Dulcina rested
In her sweet and shady bower;
Came a shepherd, and requested
In her lap to sleep an hour.
But from her look
A wound he took
So deep, that for a further boon
The nymph he prays.
Whereto she says,
Forgo me now, come to me soon.
But in vain did she conjure him
To depart her presence so;
Having a thousand tongues to allure him,
And but one to bid him go:
Where lips invite,
And eyes delight,
And cheeks, as fresh as rose in June,
Persuade delay;
What boots, she say,
Forgo me now, come to me soon?

He demands what time for pleasure
Can there be more fit than now:
She says, night gives loves that leisure,
Which the day cannot allow.
He says, the sight
Improves delight.
Which she denies: Night's murky noon
In Venus' plays
Makes bold, she says;
Forgo me now, come to me soon.

But what promise or profession
From his hands could purchase scope?
Who would sell the sweet possession
Of such beauty for a hope?
Or for the sight
Of lingering night
Forgo the present joys of noon?
Though ne'er so fair
Her speeches were,
Forgo me now, come to me soon.

How, at last, agreed these lovers?
She was fair; and he was young:
The tongue may tell what th' eye discovers;
Joys unseen are never sung.
Did she consent,
Or he relent:
Accepts he night, or grants she noon;
Left he her a maid,
Or not; she said
Forgo me now, come to me soon.

on THE LIFE OF SAINT TERESA OF AVILA
   BY HERSELF

Many of you have seen Bernini's famous sculpture of the ecstasy of Saint Teresa, and—gazing upon her divinely enraptured face—even the most hedonistic and godless among you probably thought: "Hmm, this Christian thing doesn't look so bad after all..." For while most of the Church Fathers denounced the pleasure of the flesh, it's pretty clear that Teresa de Avila, saint though she was, seemed to know a thing or two about having a good time. Truth was, she had the best of both worlds, charting her Way of Perfection while nibbling a little cake on the side. Angel's food, mind you, pure angel's food.

She was not without precedent. Other female mystics in the Middle Ages, notably Marguerite Porete of Spain and England's Margery Kempe, also experienced erotically-charged unions with the higher forces of heaven. Still, gentlemen, before we get our hopes up, I have to add that this seems to be a uniquely feminine experience: as far as I know, there aren't any accounts of medieval men getting down with the Lord or His celestial minions. In Greek mythology, of course, there were a lot of tales of higher-order beings coming down to shag the better-packaged members of humanity, but in Christianity, all the god-to-man nookie happened not in the holy writ, but in the hearts and minds of the Christians themselves. Which just goes to show a hidden component in the dynamics of sexual repression: the very force that is supposed to deny the libido becomes the object of its fantasy. Small surprise, perhaps; it's often the strictest governess who insinuates her way into our erotic dreams, regardless of what our conscious minds might dictate. In Saint Teresa's case, however, the fantastic vision is so pleasant that it utterly conceals the self-repression or violence that subtends it. Would that everyone could find such compensatory mechanisms.

from THE LIFE OF SAINT TERESA OF AVILA BY HERSELF

Our Lord was pleased at times to have me see the following vision: Beside me to my left was an angel, close at hand, in bodily form. I was not accustomed to seeing visions of this sort; they came to me very rarely. Though I frequently have visions of angels, I normally only see them as intellectual visions, as I have spoken of before. But in this case it was the Lord's will that I should see this angel in this physical manner. He was not large, but of stature rather small, and he was most beautiful. His face was afire, to say that he was one of the higher angels who seem to be made all of fire, those that we call the seraphim. They never tell me their names, but I can see that in Heaven there is a great difference between one type of angel and another, though I can't truly explain it.

In his hand he had a long spear made of gold, and at the spear's point was the burning of a fire. He appeared to me to be thrusting it into me, into my heart, then piercing into my very entrails. When he drew it back out, he seemed to draw my entrails with it, and to leave instead only the burning fire of God inside me. The pain was so great it made me moan out, and yet was of such tremendous sweetness— yes, the pain was sweet—that I would never wish it to end. The soul is satisfied within only by the presence of God. And the pain is not bodily, but spiritual, though the body has a large share in it. It is a caressing by love that occurs between the soul and God, and whoever thinks that I am lying, I can only pray that they one day feel it as well.

—TRANSLATED BY JACK MURNIGHAN

Lick the beggar's stinking feet, drink his hot urine, eat his shit and let him spit in your mouth—now are you aroused? Few of us would be, but even the most squeamish explorer into the nature of human sexuality must account for the appeal—certainly not universal—of abjection. I say "not universal" and yet, if all of our layers of libidinal repression and ignorance could suddenly be stripped away, the question might be open to dispute. Female prostitutes have told me that every man wants to be dominated; the johns who can't handle the shame of this kind of subjugation are the ones who respond with overcompensating aggression, trying to convince themselves that they are really the ones with the power. Despite popular conceptions to the contrary, the working girls insist that there are really no exceptions. And so I wonder: Is the step from submission to abjection really so great? It is clear that identity is a scratchy garment we'd all like to remove sometimes. But how to slough off the agonizing "I"? Perhaps crush it under the weight of humiliation. Bury it under a complete, boundless shame. Find transport through the boot heel licked.

Therapists would tell us paying customers that we think we deserve it. Not loving ourselves, we can't imagine other people loving us, they chant in unison. But even if this is true, there remains, to me, the question of pleasure. Is the unconscious strong enough to transform humiliation into erotic pleasure just to serve our self-hating needs? It appears so. Are we all masochists? Maybe—but not all masochists are created equal. Some figure out how to do it through sex, others through even more humbling means (in my case, grad school). These pleasures may or may not be tainted by concomitant anxieties about what precisely such tastes might mean. Some believe masochism is just pleasure, just sex (which would be what, exactly?). Others recognize it as evidence of a fault line in the psyche. Still others take pleasure in seeing it as just such a fault line: they find a masochistic delight in being able to uncover their own mechanisms, however ugly. Would that I could be so brave. Instead, I retreat into the safety of the Wonderbread sex I have known, only wondering what the unconscious actors of my desires might be staging behind the scrim.

Not so with Aleister Crowley. In his early years of writing poetry (still before the turn of the twentieth century), he privately published a book of poems entitled *White Stains*. Among them are some unflinchingly erotic explorations, the most aggressive and flamboyant of which is the bit below. Crowley enacts in his poem the scenario I described in the first line of this naughty bit. And his conclusion: that it's better than hearing angels singing at dawn. Devil's food, indeed.

Aleister Crowley's "GO INTO THE HIGHWAYS"

> Let my fond lips but drink thy golden wine,
> My bright-eyed Arab, only let me eat
> The rich brown globes of sacramental meat
> Steaming and firm, hot from their home divine,
> And let me linger with thy hands in mine,
> And lick the sweat from dainty dirty feet
> Fresh with the loose aroma of the street,
> And then anon I'll glue my mouth to thine.
> This is the height of joy, to lie and feel
> Thy spicéd spittle trickle down my throat;
> This is more pleasant than at dawn to steal
> Towards lawns and sunny brooklets, and to gloat
> Over earth's peace, and hear in the ether float
> Songs of soft spirits into rapture peal.

on THE LOVE EPISTLES OF ARISTAENETUS

O f the many stages in the heterosexual human mating ritual, my favorite might be the Everything But. When the doors of physical expression have been thrust open—all save one— the participants enter a *pas de deux* of tremendous intricacy, a push-pull negotiation that, conducted correctly, can give more pleasure than an any-point-of-entry free-for-all. Poets have long noted that restriction enhances beauty; love sonnets would be less sublime if written in free verse. Further still, restriction demands creativity, and this demand, when taken seriously, pushes the artist further than he might have gone otherwise. Longstanding couples often find that when sex, due to pregnancy or disease, becomes suddenly impossible, the myriad ways of compensating can reinvigorate what had become old hat. And thus the early-stage lover, still in the jonquil fields of courtship, should not despair when held up at third, but rejoice in the possibilities thus afforded. (Yes, those possibilities were there anyway, but who would think to slow the little engine that can?)

For men, at least, one of the prime advantages of being trapped within the Everything But is the ability to employ that potent weapon, typically exclusive to the female arsenal, The Tease. We men are normally so busy trying to fulfill our phylogenetic injunction to mate (and to prove to our fellow males that we can), that we forget how effective a bit of stalling can be. Indirection, dalliance, loitering, lingering and luxuriating are the craftsman's tools of seduction, shifting the woman into the role of the aggressor. And this is where true eroticism lies. For nothing, nothing, is sexier than enticing someone to break her own prohibitions. To have established Everything But as the policy and then to have that policy quaver under the licking flames of want. And thus, the borders of the Everything But should be traced, the possibility to transgress hinted at (obliquely), the intensity of the waiting heightened and heightened until the resiliency of the resolve jellies. And then? Well, either you do it or you don't, but the brow is sweaty either way.

Note: Apparently, not all men agree with me on the erotic power of restriction. Take this poem by the Late Classical Greek author Aristae-netus as a conspicuous counter-example.

from THE LOVE EPISTLES OF ARISTAENETUS

"Epistle XXI: Cruel Companion"

The god of the love-darting bow,
Whose bliss is man's heart to destroy,
Oft contrives to embitter our woe
By a specious resemblance of joy.
Long—long had Architeles sought
The fair Telesippe to gain:
She coolly his passion denied
Yet seem'd somewhat moved at his pain.
At length she consented to hear;
But 'twas done with a view to beguile:
For her terms were most harsh and severe,
And a frown was as good as her smile.
"You may freely," says she, "touch my breast,
And kiss, while a kiss has its charms;
And (provided I am not undrest)
Encircle me round in your arms.
In short, any favor you please,
But expect not, nor think of the last:
Lest enraged I revoke my decrees,
And your sentence of exile be cast."—
"Be it so," cried the youth, with delight,
"Thy pleasure, my fair one, is mine:

Since I'm blest as a prince at your sight,
Sure to touch thee, will make me divine.
But why keep one favor alone,
And grant such a number beside?"—
"Because the men value the boon
But only so long as denied.
They seek it with labor and pain;
When gain'd, throw it quickly away:
For youth is unsettled and vain,
And its choice scarce persists for a day."
—Thus pines the poor victim away,
forced to nibble and starve on a kiss.
Serve worse than e'en eunuchs—for they
Can never feel torture like this.

—TRANSLATED BY RICHARD BRINSLEY SHERIDAN,
MODIFIED BY JACK MURNIGHAN

There is a tendency among young writers to construct sentences simply for the sake of using one of their favorite words. I used to do this all the time; any chance I had to make something an *autochthon*, any time a *catafalque* might be erected, anything that could be colored *puce* or slide down a *sluice* or have to *vamoose* was good enough for me to bend my plot around it, Aristotelian unities be damned. This is not the sign of a good writer. But at a certain point, like many of the young, I saw the error of my ways and started editing out each and every sentence with any of the above words in it.

I will admit, however, that the above paragraph enacts a kind of *apophasis* (another favorite word!)—claiming I'm not going to talk about something and, in the process of not doing so, managing to talk about it anyway. In telling you I stopped using my favorite words, I found an excuse to use them—and so many! But, in fact, that's what this introduction is all about. For the problem, you see, is that the literary selection I've chosen allows me to use one of my all-time favorite words: *polyorchid*. Polyorchid, polyorchid, polyorchid, polyorchid, polyorchid, polyorchid...

Polyorchid—someone who has more than two testicles—is not a word you get to throw around every day. In college, there was a guy famous for having three testicles (and blue hair), and one of my friends had to become a monoorchid some years back (a rather traumatic experience for him; I decided against sending him a box of Uniball pens)... but it is still rare for polyorchids to come up in conversation, or to appear in any kind of decent literature. Pity.

And thus my amusement when I stumbled on this brief narrative in Guillaume Apollinaire's *The Eleven Thousand Virgins*, one of the

pornographic books he wrote for money at the beginning of the twentieth century. Despite Apollinaire's ample poetic gifts (he penned the
excellent volume *Alcools*), his contract smut is little better than any of
the prurient pamphlets or "collector's edition" erotica one could get
from the Victorian period on. But the scene below, a classic case of
amorously assumed (and briefly mistaken) identity, has a nice twist
when the lover proves to have a mere two testicles. There are a lot of
literary examples of women not being able to tell who they are having
sex with in the dark (not a good sign, I take it), but Apollinaire's is a
comical exception. In this case, it takes more than two to tango.

from Guillaume Apollinaire's
THE ELEVEN THOUSAND VIRGINS

"The proverbial wine is opened, and now we must drink it. Let us
continue our explorations."

He opened another door, which closed itself behind him. He
found himself in a room even darker than the first.

A soft female voice said in French: "Is that you, Fedor?"

"Yes, it's me, my love!" replied Mony in a low but resolute
voice. His heart was pounding enough to break through his chest.

He advanced rapidly toward where the voice had come from
and stumbled into a bed. There was a woman lying on it, fully
clothed. She embraced Mony passionately, darting her tongue into
his mouth. He responded to her caresses. He lifted up her skirts. She
parted her thighs. Her legs were bare and a delicious perfume of ver-
bena emanated from her satiny skin, mingled with the perfume of
her odor of woman. Her cunt, where Mony placed his hand, was
damp. She murmured:

"Let's fuck. I can't wait any longer. Wicked man, it's been
eight days since you've come to see me."

But Mony, instead of replying, had brought out his menacing
cock, fully armed, climbed on the bed and went to stick his angry

sword into the hairy crevice of this unknown woman, who immediately began to wiggle her thighs saying:

"Put it in all the way. You're making me come!"

At the same time, she put her hand at the base of the member that was inside her and began to stroke the two little balls which serve as appendages and are known as testicles not, as is commonly supposed, because they testify to the consummation of the act of love, but rather because they are little heads (testae) which contain the cervical matter whence force spurts out the lower intelligence, just as the head contains the brain, which is the seat of mental functions.

The hand of the unknown woman delicately explored Mony's balls. All of a sudden, she let out a cry and, with a twist of her ass, dislodged the ravisher.

"Monsieur!" she cried, "you have deceived me. My lover has three!"

She leapt off the bed, flipped an electric switch and the light came on.

—TRANSLATED BY JACK MURNIGHAN

CHARLES BAUDELAIRE

t a particular moment in the otherwise forgettable Catherine Breillat film, *Romance*, the female lead picks up a man on the street, takes him back to her apartment building and has sex with him on the stairwell. All of a sudden, however, the sex becomes rape, and the man runs off taunting her: "I fucked your ass! I fucked your ass!" It's a disturbing scene on many fronts (not least as part of the surprisingly anti-sex sentiment that runs through the film), but it made me conscious again of how much the ideas of having and taking are bound up in sexual relations, despite whatever kindness and gentleness we might like to prevail.

I am speaking, of course, about the hackneyed conception of sex as pursuit and evasion, a function of one party conquering the other, and, in doing so, managing to assert their power (normally thought to be from male to female, though the reverse is sometimes just as true). All sexual relations do not correspond to this model, obviously, but I have noticed that many men will respond to a sexily dressed or exceptionally beautiful woman by saying they want to fuck her—not, it seems, out of actual desire, but out of a violent urge to bring her down a peg. Sex is a vehicle, at times, for expressing frustration and self-hatred, for the feeling of impotence in the face of the unattainable, for the accumulated exhaustion many men feel with the whole process of pursuit itself and the desire to punish women both for having evaded and, at the critical juncture, for actually having succumbed.

And yet, Breillat's scene allows us to recognize a further subtlety: that what counts as having or taking someone will differ from person to person, and perhaps from circumstance to circumstance. Conventionally, men have women when there's sex; women have men when there's a ring (though it's clear that this conception is aging). Breillat's rapist, however, needed anal sex to feel like he had *had* the protagonist.

By contrast, I once wrote a character who wanted only to taste a woman's vagina; sex wasn't necessary for him to feel he had had her— only taste. It's clear that any number of other lines could be drawn, all arbitrary.

It would be nice to be able to tease out which sexual motivations derive from erotic desire, and which from the violent wish to seize power. I think a lot of sex has elements of both, and it might not always be clear what the mix is. In the excerpt below, Baudelaire is describing the moon-touched woman who appears and reappears in his *Paris Spleen*, a collection of prose poems written about *fin de siècle* Paris. By the end, it becomes clear that he is trying to differentiate his true feelings for her from the simple desire to conquer. Perhaps here, Baudelaire too recognizes the contrary impulses that can underlay lust and wants to insist not on violence, but on beauty. Would that the balance could always shift so.

from Charles Baudelaire's PARIS SPLEEN

"The Desire of the Painter"

Unhappy, perhaps, the man, but happy the artist shattered by desire!

I burn to paint her who to me appeared so rarely and fled so quickly, like a beautiful thing regrettably left behind by the traveler and swept into the night. How long ago that she disappeared!

She is beautiful, and more than beautiful; she is surprising. In her, blackness abounds, and everything she inspires is nocturnal and profound. Her eyes are two caves scintillating vaguely with mystery, and her gaze shines like lightning: an explosion in the shadows.

I might compare her to a black sun, if one could imagine a black star pouring forth light and happiness. But with her it is easier to think of the moon, which probably marked her with her fearsome influence. Not the white moon of idyllic romance, which resembles a frigid bride, but a sinister and intoxicating moon, suspended deep in a stormy night and jostled by hastening clouds. Not the peaceful and discreet moon attending upon the sleep of the innocent, but a moon ripped from the sky, defeated and rebellious, which the Witches of Thessaly fiercely compel to dance on the terrified grass!

On her little brow rest a stubborn will and the love of prey. However, below her disquieting face, where mobile nostrils breathe in the unknown and the impossible, with inexpressible grace, bursts forth the laughter of a large mouth, red and white, and delicious, making one dream of the miracle of a superb blossom budding in volcanic ground.

There are women who inspire the desire to defeat them and take one's pleasure from them; but this woman creates only the desire to die slowly under her gaze.

—TRANSLATED BY JACK MURNIGHAN

on OUR LADY OF THE FLOWERS   JEAN GENET

few weeks ago I made the terrible mistake of reading a novel that's become a cause célèbre in France, *The Elementary Particles* by Michel Houellebecq (pronounced WELL-beck). The book has been getting a lot of press for its blend of supposedly racy sex and hard science, first in France where it sold over 300,000 copies, then here and elsewhere abroad (it's being translated into twelve languages). But contrary to the hype, it's no *Gravity's Rainbow*—on either the sexual or scientific front—nor even worth the slightest *hors*-France hubbub. In fact, the only thing at all radical about the book is that it's so unabashed in its misogyny.

Houellebecq, who lives with his mother, is clearly not a well man (judging not only from the novel, but from the way he propositioned—in the most vulgar way—a *New York Times Magazine* journalist who came to interview him). One can only assume that the frustrated adolescent science student bitterness that marks his characters' relations to women is a reflection of a long-stewed rancor of his own. Reading *The Elementary Particles*, I kept thinking that it was very much like *A Confederacy of Dunces*, only without the humor—not unlike the woman about whom Oscar Wilde remarked, "She resembled a peacock in everything but beauty."

So why all the spilled ink, the sales and the busy-bee translators? Because France needs a voice for its would-be bad-boy self. It wants its own Bukowski (having more or less stolen ours), and, more than that, it wants another Genet. Yes, Genet. Genet both blessed and cursed France with his gallows humor and gallows sexuality, his generic indifference and his utter disregard for the class of people who came to champion him. I live in Chinatown and eat out a lot; sometimes, I have to confess, authenticity becomes a bit much. Genet can require as strong a stomach as pork blood congee, though the literary elite of France would love to

pretend that he's precisely their taste, that his incarcerated voice channels their bourgeois angst. It doesn't, and he would have spat thickly on
most anyone he saw reading him in the metro. And yet the French per-
sist, seeking proxies for their fantasized rebellion, thus accounting for
why poor facsimiles like Houellebecq pass as well as they do.
Houellebecq, peon that he is, is the closest they've had in quite a while.
He is still incredibly weak by comparison. Here is the real thing.

from Jean Genet's OUR LADY OF THE FLOWERS

The newspapers are tattered by the time they reach my cell, and the
finest pages have been looted of their finest flowers, those pimps, like
gardens in May. The big, inflexible, strict pimps, their members in full
bloom—I no longer know whether they are lilies or whether lilies and
members are not totally they, so much so that in the evening, on my
knees, in thought, I encircle their legs with my arms—all that rigidity
floors me and makes me confuse them, and the memory which I gladly
give as food for my nights is of yours, which, as I caressed it, remained
inert, stretched out; only your rod, unsheathed and brandished, went
through my mouth with the suddenly cruel sharpness of a steeple
puncturing a cloud of ink, a hatpin a breast. You did not move, you
were not asleep, you were not dreaming, you were in flight, motion-
less and pale, frozen, straight, stretched out stiff on the flat bed, like a
coffin on the sea, and I know that we were chaste, while I, in all attention, felt you flow into me, warm and white, in continuous little jerks.
Perhaps you were playing at coming. At the climax, you were lit up
with a quiet ecstasy, which enveloped your blessed body in a supernat-
ural nimbus, like a cloak that you pierce with your head and feet.

—TRANSLATED BY BERNARD FRECHTMAN

on REMEMBRANCE OF THINGS PAST

MARCEL PROUST

kay, I'm going to say it right now: I read the whole thing. I really did. All 3,400+ pages or however long it is—I read every tortured, reflective, tactile, teeming, overstuffed, static, stick-in-the-mud, plotless page of Marcel Proust's eight-volume *Remembrance of Things Past*. (In English, mind you. And from what I hear, the Pléiade editors of the French edition recently saw fit to add another couple hundred pages. *Sacre bleu...*) I read the whole thing, and like a lot of other long books people tend not to read in their entirety—the Bible, *Moby Dick*, *Gravity's Rainbow*, *The Faerie Queene*—*Remembrance of Things Past* has a fair amount of sex in it. Not exactly your Fabio ravishes Guinevere kind of raciness, more Proustian, i.e. more recollected, more quiet and cork-lined (like the room he shut himself up in for much of his later life), and, let's call a spade a spade, more repressed. For Marcel, despite his numerous narratives of dallying with the fairer sex, was himself the fairest of all, the most fey, the most effete (he is even described this way in the book). And though he doesn't take out a billboard in *Remembrance* to tell you that he's gay, he does about everything else to make it clear.

Proust's predominate method of tipping you off to his sexuality is his insistence on the Takes One to Know One–ness of being gay. For if Swinburne is the great Poet of the Hickey, then Proust is the consummate Chronicler of Gaydar. Maybe that's not the most fitting title for the preeminent French novelist of the twentieth century, but Proust dedicates over a quarter of *Remembrance* to his investigation of homosexuality, and the topic of how gays meet each other is one of his sustained obsessions. In a particularly extended passage, he likens the ability of gays to identify one another and meet despite all odds and impediments as akin to the miracle of certain "precious plants," incapable of fertilizing on their own, who only by "providential hazard" come across the "unlikely insect...to visit the neglected pistil." A particularly rare hothouse flower, Proust—one can only imagine what kind of insect would have been necessary for his blossom.

But in the encounter below, such a meeting does take place, thanks only to the subtleties of gaydar—described in every detail by Proust—that allow so insignificant a thing as a hand movement seen at a distance to be the critical shibboleth bespeaking compatibility. It concerns a nobleman and a social-climbing tailor; they meet in the tailor's shop and Proust watches the whole thing from the rafters above. In the greatest book about human perception, the greatest testament to detachment and reflection, it is only fitting that the protagonist witnesses the sex, not smelling the sweat and feeling the bodies from within, but seeing and hearing it all from a passive distance. For Proust, the only life is the life of the mind, and reality rarely intrudes.

from Marcel Proust's REMEMBRANCE OF THINGS PAST

Based on the series of inarticulate sounds that I heard the first time in Jupien's rooms, I imagine that few words had been exchanged. It is true that these sounds were so violent that, if they had not always been accompanied an octave higher by a corresponding plaint I might have been able to believe that one person was slitting another's throat within a few feet of me, and that subsequently the murderer and his resuscitated victim were taking a bath to wash away the traces of the crime. From this, I concluded some time later that there is another thing just as clamorous as suffering, namely pleasure, especially when there is added to it—lacking the threat of conceiving a child in the process, which obviously could not be the case here (despite the hardly credible instance in the *Golden Legend*)—any immediate concern about safety. Finally, after about half an hour of this (during which time I had progressively hoisted myself up a ladder so as to peep through the fanlight which I did not open), a conversation started up between them. Jupien adamantly refused the money that the Baron was attempting to give to him.

—TRANSLATED BY JACK MURNIGHAN

on RUBYFRUIT JUNGLE

RITA MAE BROWN

During the 2000 Republican presidential primary race, I got a call from a journalist asking about John McCain. The decorated pilot had apparently just expressed alarm that there were computers in public libraries that kids could use to access pornography. The journalist had called me because, as the erstwhile editor of *Nerve*, he thought I would defend freedom on the Internet against conservative politicians seeking to restrict it. Instead, I said that if John McCain didn't know how to find pornography in a library without a computer then I'd be happy to give him a tour. Or, better yet, ask any thirteen-year-old kid for a helping hand.

Even in junior high most of us knew how to find our way around the stacks, from the art nude books in the photography section to the genitalia chapters in anatomy manuals to novels like *Rubyfruit Jungle* or *Deenie* to anthropological spreads in *National Geographic*. What McCain didn't realize is that porn isn't just triple-X pictures, it's whatever works for whomever is using it. The harder it is to lay your hands on, the better it is. A little work, as Saint Augustine said about reading the Bible, makes it a lot more interesting.

Well, many years have passed since I was thirteen, but it's clear that my reading habits haven't changed that much. I'm still going to the library to get my jollies, but those jollies—hopefully—have gotten a little more sophisticated. Which inevitably means that the pleasures of such books as Rita Mae Brown's 1973 novel *Rubyfruit Jungle* are more nostalgic than actual. But no matter, Brown made the bold step of including lesbian (and straight) sex in a breezy coming-of-age novel; in doing so, she showed a generation of women just how normal and legitimate woman-to-woman desire is. If it seems a little dated now, it's only because none of us is thirteen anymore, and we know our way around the library a bit better.

Holly lived on West End Avenue in a big apartment with lots of old molding on the ceilings and parquet floors. A monstrous silver Persian, Gertrude Stein, greeted us at the door and she was pissed that Holly stayed out so late. On our journey through the apartment we found a trail of feline discontent: a chewed slipper, a shredded corner of the rug, and when we passed the bathroom we saw that Gertrude Stein had pulled the entire roll of toilet paper off the roller.

"Is she always this vindictive?"

"Yes, but then I look forward to her little surprises. You know, of course, that we are heading toward the bedroom and that we're going in there to make love?"

"I know."

"Then why are you walking so slow? Come on, run." Holly trotted into a bedroom boasting an enormous brass bed with a plush maroon bedspread. Halfway to the bed, she had her blouse off. "Hurry up."

"I'm going slow so as to not arouse Gertrude's suspicion in case she's the jealous type." Sure enough, Gertrude was paddling after me with hostility in her slanted eyes.

"You're safe. Gerty will only try to slither between us."

"Wonderful. I've never done it with a cat before." Holly had all her clothes off and was rolling down the bedspread. She was more beautiful out of her clothes than in them. I tripped getting out of my pants.

"Molly, you really should dance. You're all sinew and muscle and you look terrific. Come here."

She pulled me on the bed and I was close to passing out from being next to six feet of smooth flesh. She was running her fingers through my hair, biting my neck, and I started floating on hot energy. She had a soft, thick afro which she slid all over my body. And she kept biting me. Her tongue ran along the back of my ear, into my ear, down my neck, along my shoulder bone and on down to my breasts, then back up to my mouth. I lost track of linear sequence after that, but I know she put the full weight of her body on top of mine and I thought I was going to scream she felt so fine. I ran my hands down her back and could barely reach her behind she was so long. Each time she moved I could feel the muscles under her skin fluidly changing shape. The woman was a demon. She started slow and got wilder and wilder until she was holding me so tight I couldn't breathe and I didn't care. I could feel her inside me, outside me, all over me; I didn't know where her body began and mine left off. One of us was yelling but I don't know who it was or what she was yelling. Hours later we untangled ourselves to notice that the sun was high over the Hudson, snow was falling in the river and Gertrude had devoured my right shoe, my only pair.

on A CLOCKWORK ORANGE ANTHONY BURGESS

hichever way you fall on the issue of nature versus nurture, it's hard to deny the power of *a posteriori* conditioning. What's true of Pavlov's dogs tends to be true of mammals as a whole—including humans. Nowhere are the implications of behavioral conditioning drawn out with more chilling implications than in Anthony Burgess's dystopian near-future nightmare, *A Clockwork Orange*. The antihero protagonist Alex, having murdered and raped his way through adolescence, is forced to watch similar actions on film until the very sight of violence or nudity makes him retch. As in *Brave New World*, Burgess's all-too-imaginable "state" exhibits a level of social control that has the power to remove the humanity from its citizens, for better and worse. *A Clockwork Orange* makes clear that whatever the source of our actions, choice (illusional or not) is what makes us who we are.

In this scene, Alex is up to his usual tricks, coercing two schoolgirls he meets at a record store to come home with him for some Beethoven and a little of the old "in-and-out." Burgess's great achievement in the book is to sheathe a level of violence we are truly unaccustomed to seeing (on page or screen) within an invented yet recognizable new slang. Odd as the *Clockwork* idiom is, we manage to understand it. And perhaps an even greater accomplishment—we recognize its implications for the future. Will we heed the warning?

from Anthony Burgess's A CLOCKWORK ORANGE

These two young ptitsas were much alike, though not sisters. They had the same ideas or lack of, and the same colour hair—a like dyed strawy. Well, they would grow up real today. Today I would make a day of it. No school this afterlunch, but education certain, Alex as teacher. Their names, they said, were Marty and Sonietta, bezoomny enough and in the heighth of their childish fashion, so I said:

"Righty right, Marty and Sonietta. Time for the big spin. Come."...

What was actually done that afternoon there is no need to describe, brothers, as you may easily guess all. Those two were unplattied and smecking fit to crack in no time at all, and they thought it the bolshiest fun to viddy old Uncle Alex standing there all nagoy and pan-handled, squirting the hypodermic like some bare doctor, then giving myself the old jab of growling jungle-cat secretion in the rooker. Then I pulled the lovely Ninth out of its sleeve, so that Ludwig van was now nagoy too, and I set the needle hissing on to the last movement, which was all bliss. There it was then, the bass strings like govoreeting away from under my bed at the rest of the orchestra, and then the male human goloss coming in and telling them all to be joyful, and then the lovely blissful tune all about Joy being a glorious spark like of heaven and then I felt the old tigers leap in me and then I leapt on these two young ptitsas. This time they thought nothing fun and stopped creeching with high mirth, and had to submit to the strange and weird desires of Alexander the Large which, what with the Ninth and the hypo jab, were choodessny and zammechat and very demanding, O my brothers. But they were both very very drunken and could hardly feel very much.

When the last movement had gone round for the second time with all the banging and creeching about Joy Joy Joy Joy, then these two young ptitsas were not acting the big lady sophisto no more. They were like waking up to what was being done to their malenky persons and saying that they wanted to go home and like I was a wild beast. They looked like they had been in some big bitva, as indeed they had, and were all bruised and pouty. Well, if they would not go to school they must still have their education. And education they had had. They were creeching and going ow ow ow as they put their platties on, and they were like punchipunching me with their teeny fists as I lay there dirty and nagoy and fair shagged and fagged on the bed. This young Sonietta was creeching: "Beast and hateful animal. Filthy horror." So I let them get their things together and get out, which they did, talking about how the rozzes should be got on to me and all that cal. Then they were going down the stairs and I dropped off to sleep, still with the old Joy Joy Joy Joy crashing and howling away.

y innocence got swiped rather late. It was already the summer after my senior year of high school before I first had sex, but thinking back, that's not the event I would point to as the moment of my fall. No, innocence lost is not so much a function of an external thing like getting laid, but of an internal condition or mutation, most likely the recognition of a ferocity of desire that had never shown its face before. Or, in my case, the recognition of the ferocious desire of another that finally clued me in to the glories of the female libido—and raised the stakes to a height from which they'd never descend.

She was a college girl visiting from Chicago; I was the unsuspecting hayseed providing local color, ready rube for a rustic romp. I don't know if she guessed my age: with my adolescent acne, postpunk bob haircut and underfed sapling torso, I could have passed for thirteen. But I was seventeen, and more than a little terrified by the idea of a girl in her twenties. And a girl-terror she was: blonde, bouncing, brash, freckled, Chicago-Irish . . . with all the confidence and volume that goes with it. As I remember it, one minute we were dancing, the music was loud but she was even louder, and then she was *insisting*. And I was like a stranger to the customs, or at least to the language: I didn't know why we were going outside, I didn't know why her lips were on mine, why her hand was in my pants, why my bare ass was on the grass, and why, oh why, her lips were on . . .

And at that moment my innocence, uncaged dove, lofted skyward, not to return. It clicked: all of it, all at once.

This excerpt is a similar tale of theft. The boy hero is the young protagonist Ambrosio of Matthew Lewis's fabulous late eighteenth-century Gothic novel *The Monk*. In a certain sense, the entire novel is about the loss of innocence—or the slide, as it were, once it begins. Here is the critical first step: seduction at the hands of Matilda.

from Matthew Lewis's **THE MONK**

"Live for me, Matilda; for me and gratitude"—(He caught her hand, and pressed it rapturously to his lips.)—"Remember our late conversations; I now consent to every thing. Remember in what lively colours you described the union of souls; be it ours to realize those ideas. Let us forget the distinctions of sex, despise the world's prejudices, and only consider each other as brother and friend. Live, then, Matilda, oh! Live for me!"

"Ambrosio, it must not be. When I thought thus, I deceived both you and myself: either I must die at present, or expire by the lingering torments of unsatisfied desire. Oh! Since we last conversed together, a dreadful veil has been rent from my eyes. I love you no longer with the devotion which is paid to a saint; I prize you no more for the virtues of your soul; I lust for the enjoyment of your person. The woman reigns in my bosom, and I am become prey to the wildest of passions. Away with friendship! 'Tis a cold unfeeling word: my bosom burns with love, with unutterable love, and love must be its return. Tremble then, Ambrosio, tremble to succeed in your prayers. If I live, your truth, your reputation, your reward of a life past in sufferings, all that you value, is irretrievably lost. I shall no longer be able to combat my passions, shall seize every opportunity to excite your desires, and labour to effect your dishonour and my own. No, no, Ambrosio, I must not live; I am convinced with every moment that I have but one alternative; I feel with every heartthrob, that I must enjoy you or die."

"Amazement! Matilda! Can it be you who speak to me?"

He made a movement as if to quit his seat. She uttered a loud shriek, and, raising herself half out of the bed, threw her arms round the friar to detain him.

"Oh! Do not leave me! Listen to my errors with compassion: in a few hours I shall be no more: yet a little, and I am free from this disgraceful passion."

"Wretched woman, what can I say to you? I cannot—I must not—But live, Matilda! Oh, live!"

"You do not reflect on what you ask. What? Live to plunge myself in infamy? To become the agent of hell? To work the destruction both of you and of myself? Feel this heart, father."

She took his hand. Confused, embarrassed, and fascinated, he withdrew it not, and felt her heart throb under it.

"Feel this heart, father! It is yet the seat of honour, truth, and chastity: if it beats tomorrow, it must fall a prey to the blackest crimes. Oh, let me then die today! Let me die while I yet deserve the tears of the virtuous. Thus will I expire!"—(She reclined her head upon his shoulder; her golden hair poured itself over his chest.)—"Folded in your arms, I shall sink to sleep; your hand shall close my eyes forever, and your lips receive my dying breath. And will you not sometimes think of me? Will you not sometimes shed a tear upon my tomb? Oh, yes, yes, yes! That kiss is my assurance."

The hour was night. All was silence around. The faint beams of a solitary lamp darted upon Matilda's figure, and shed through the chamber a dim, mysterious light. No prying eye or curious ear was near the lovers: nothing was heard but Matilda's melodious accents. Ambrosio was in the full vigour of manhood; he saw before him a young and beautiful woman, the preserver of his life, the adorer of his person; and whom affection for him had reduced to the brink of the grave. He sat upon her bed; his hand rested upon her bosom; her head reclined voluptuously upon his breast. Who then can wonder if he yielded to the temptation? Drunk with desire, he pressed his lips to those which sought them; his kisses vied with Matilda's in warmth and passion: he clasped her rapturously in his arms; he forgot his vows, his sanctity, and his fame; he remembered nothing but the pleasure and opportunity.

"Ambrosio! Oh, my Ambrosio!" sighed Matilda.

"Thine, ever thine," murmured the friar, and sunk upon her bosom.

on PASSION AND BETRAYAL   GENNIFER FLOWERS

𝕴t's a general principle with naughty bits—as with cathedrals, provolone and lovers—that older is better. And so with a not-insubstantial grudge must I occasionally admit that there is a present out there to complement the past, and a vast, teeming realm of the "timely." Now the timely, being at odds with the universal and eternal, is the most pejorative adjective in a philosopher's lexicon, while being the bread and butter of the magazine and newspaper worlds (and pretty much everybody else's). So even if in my heart of hearts I would like to be running an athenaeum, I live in the world of contemporary publishing, and thus there is a time or place for everything to which I must attend.

I, like many, was saddened by the election of the latest Bush. It's clear the new guy will provide fewer naughty bits than the old Arkansan billy goat with all his malfeasance. Even if Bill Clinton wasn't particularly good for America (and its daughters), he was good for the erotica lobby. During the Clinton administration, I wrote about the Starr Report in all its Dragnet-meets-Lady Chatterley glory, but now that the come-stain presidency is a thing of the past, and the collective remembrance of it is slowly eroding, like morals, with each passing year, I think enough time has passed that I can dip again into the oval well and see how dirty I can get my hand.

And so, for those of you with insufficiently inquiring minds to have bought the mass-market hardback *Passion and Betrayal* by Gennifer Flowers, I dutifully reproduce one of its many piquant descriptions of then-Guvna Bill. He wasn't yet the most powerful man in the world, nor its most famous analinguist, but the seeds are there. Ready for blooms.

I had barely closed the door behind him before he pulled me into his arms and began kissing me. All that sexual tension that had been relentlessly building for weeks in both of us suddenly erupted. A desire far beyond a physical attraction overwhelmed me. Everything about this man excited me: his brain, his charm and his incredible sexuality.

We stumbled toward the bedroom, ripping off our clothes as we went, reluctant to release each other long enough to step out of them...

As a lover, Bill was great! Though not particularly well endowed, his desire to please was astounding. He was determined to satisfy me, and boy did he! At times I thought my head would explode with the pleasure. This was more than great sex, it was great everything; I was falling in love with Bill Clinton, inside and out...

We spent two or three hours together, mostly making love. During our short breathers, he would hold me and stroke my hair. He was so sweet and tender. It was as if I were the only one who existed for him at that moment...

His stamina amazed me. We made love over and over that night, and he never seemed to run out of energy. Had he stayed with me the entire night, I have no doubt he could have kept going 'til dawn. But spending the night was out of the question: Bill had a wife to go home to.

on DRACULA BRAM STOKER

Under normal circumstances, being alone in a room with three nymphomaniacal hotties is not an unwelcome condition. Rum thing, then, when you happen to be in Transylvania, and the bite marks they want to leave on your neck are not the garden-variety hickey. But welcome to the world of Bram Stoker's *Dracula*, by which I mean Bram Stoker's novel *Dracula*, not the schmaltzy film of the same name that gave Keanu Reeves another chance to see how little emotion he could convey on the silver screen.

Films rarely live up to the books they are based on, but Coppola's *Dracula* was a pointedly bad case. (It seems that when a film includes the author's name in the title it's doomed: take lovely Leo in the production they felt the need to call *William Shakespeare's Romeo and Juliet*. Oh, you mean THAT *Romeo and Juliet*!) But it's an easy thing to criticize celluloid adaptations, and a healthy, generous brain has to find ways to be more constructive. So I will only say that the *Dracula* you can carry to the beach is a wonderfully scary, sexy, surprising book. It's a shame, in a sense, that horror fiction is now such a lowbrow, glossy paperback genre (despite Steven King's prolific brilliance), for Stoker's achievement holds up against the best of his *fin de siècle* peers. *Dracula* might be scary, but it's also literature par excellence.

from Bram Stoker's DRACULA

I suppose I must have fallen asleep; I hope so, but I fear, for all that followed was startlingly real—so real that now, sitting here in the broad, full sunlight of the morning, I cannot in the least believe that it was all sleep.

I was not alone. The room was the same, unchanged in any way since I came into it; I could see along the floor, in the brilliant moonlight, my own footsteps marked where I had disturbed the long accumulation of dust. In the moonlight opposite me were three young women, ladies by their dress and manner. I thought at the time that I must be dreaming when I saw them, for, though the moonlight was behind them, they threw no shadow on the floor. They came close to me and looked at me for some time, and then whispered together. Two were dark, and had high aquiline noses, like the Count, and great dark, piercing eyes that seemed to be almost red when contrasted with the pale yellow moon. The other was fair, as fair as can be, with great, wavy masses of golden hair and eyes like pale sapphires. I seemed somehow to know her face, and to know it in connection with some dreamy fear, but I could not recollect at the moment how or where. All three had brilliant white teeth that shone like pearls against the ruby of their voluptuous lips. There was something about them that made me uneasy, some longing and at the same time some deadly fear. I felt in my heart a wicked, burning desire that they would kiss me with those red lips. It is not good to note this down, lest some day it should meet Mina's eyes and cause her pain; but it is the truth. They whispered together, and then they all three laughed—such a silvery, musical laugh, but as hard as though the sound never could have come through the softness of human lips. It was like the intolerable, tingling sweetness of water-glasses when played on by a cunning hand. The fair girl shook her head coquettishly, and the other two urged her on. One said:

"Go on! You are first, and we shall follow; yours is the right to begin." The other added:

"He is young and strong; there are kisses for us all." I lay quiet, looking out under my eyelashes in an agony of delightful anticipation. The fair girl advanced and bent over me till I could feel the movement of her breath upon me. Sweet it was in one sense, honey-sweet, and sent the same tingling through the nerves as her voice, but with a bitter underlying the sweet, a bitter offensiveness, as one smells in blood.

I was afraid to raise my eyelids, but looked out and saw perfectly under the lashes. The fair girl went on her knees, and bent over me, fairly gloating. There was a deliberate voluptuousness which was both thrilling and repulsive, and as she arched her neck she actually licked her lips like an animal, till I could see in the moonlight the moisture shining on the scarlet lips and on the red tongue as it lapped the white sharp teeth. Lower and lower went her head as the lips went below the range of my mouth and chin and seemed about to fasten on my throat. Then she paused, and I could hear the churning sound of her tongue as it licked her teeth and lips, and could feel the hot breath on my neck. Then the skin of my throat began to tingle as one's flesh does when the hand that is to tickle it approaches nearer—nearer. I could feel the soft, shivering touch of the lips on the supersensitive skin of my throat, and the hard dents of two sharp teeth, just touching and pausing there. I closed my eyes in a languorous ecstasy and waited—waited with beating heart.

But at that instant another sensation swept through me as quick as lightning. I was conscious of the presence of the Count, and of his being as if lapped in a storm of fury. As my eyes opened involuntarily I saw his strong hand grasp the slender neck of the fair woman and with giant's power draw it back, the blue eyes transformed with fury, the white teeth champing with rage, and the fair cheeks blazing red with passion. But the Count! Never did I imagine such wrath and fury, even to the demons of the pit. His eyes were positively blazing. The red light in them was lurid, as if the flames of hell-fire blazed behind them. His face was deathly pale, and the lines of it were hard like drawn wires; the thick eyebrows that met over the nose now seemed like a heaving bar of white-hot metal. With a fierce sweep of his arm, he hurled the woman from him, and then motioned to the others, as though he were beating them back; it was the same imperious gesture that I had seen used to the wolves. In a voice which, though low and almost in a whisper, seemed to cut through the air and then ring round the room as he said:

"How dare you touch him, any of you? How dare you cast eyes on him when I had forbidden it? Back, I tell you all! This man belongs to me!"

on "THE 400-POUND CEO"   GEORGE SAUNDERS

've never been fat—oh no, quite the reverse. My age outpaced my waist-size a few years back, but it took thirty-one years to get to that point. Having had the misfortune of skipping a year of elementary school, combined with congenital tendencies toward late blooming, all through my childhood I found myself playing a grim kind of catch-up with my classmates in the all-too-crucial game of pituitary development. Certain moments remain crystalline in my memory: in fifth grade I weighed fifty pounds; my closest friend weighed exactly double. In seventh grade, everyone in my class had to write their weight on a slip of paper so the teacher could calculate the mean. When he read mine, seventy-nine pounds (the seven crossed German-style), he said out loud, "Okay, who's screwing around?" I raised my hand, said that that was my real weight and was called to the front to get on the scale. Consummate shame—seventy-seven. I entered high school weighing ninety-three. Word got around, and one day I was pulled out of my advanced math class by the wrestling coach to be on the varsity team. Most schools have no one to compete in the ninety-eight-pound class and have to forfeit matches. Just my presence guaranteed victory; I would have lettered. But, still prepubescent, I was unwilling to shower with the team after practice, and their creepy insistence compelled me to quit after three days.

It is clear, though, that however traumatic it is to be stalk-thin and muscleless in your average American high school, it's better than being on the other end of the scale. Extreme skinniness is often outgrown, as in my case when I gained twenty-five pounds in my senior year of high school. But fat generally stays, and the overeating/low self-image/overeating cycle is well documented. Nor does society respond similarly to the excessively light and the excessively heavy: skinny people can often get away with it, but if you're fat, you are considered the last legitimate target of hatred and bigotry, and kids, like the parents who teach them, can be merciless.

Nor does the torture end at graduation. I think we could all guess, if we bothered to take a minute to do so, how difficult it must be to be obese and still bear the full complement of human desire. But few of us take the time; it's easier just to think that it's the fat person's fault, as if the complexity of psychological dynamics, including self-hatred (which afflicts us all in different ways), was an easy thing to tease out. The excerpt below, from George Saunders's deservedly famous short story "The 400-Pound CEO," lets us into the mind and heart of just such a man, and lets us feel the awesome weight of his disappointment. Sexual desire has, at times, been a profoundly difficult and painful part of most of our lives; what's poignant in Saunders's creation is how, even for the least attractive of men, the frailest crocus of hope breaks through the ice of universal scorn.

from George Saunders's "THE 400-POUND CEO"

When I've finished invoicing I enjoy a pecan cluster. Two, actually. Claude comes in all dirty from the burial and sees me snacking and feels compelled to point out that even my sub-rolls have sub-rolls. He's right but still it isn't nice to say. Tim asks did Claude make that observation after having wild sex with me all night. That's a comment I'm not fond of. But Tim's the boss. His T-shirt says: I HOLD YOUR PURSE STRINGS IN MY HOT LITTLE HAND.

"Ha, ha, Tim," says Claude. "I'm no homo. But if I was one, I'd die before doing it with Mr. Lard."

"Ha, ha," says Tim. "Good one. Isn't that a good one, Jeffrey?"

"That's a good one," I say glumly.

What a bitter little office.

My colleagues leave hippo refrigerator magnets on my seat. They imply that I'm a despondent virgin, which I'm not. They might change their tune if they ever spoke with Ellen Burtomly regarding the beautiful night we spent at her brother Bob's cottage. I was by no means slim then but could at least buy pants off the rack and walk from the den to the kitchen without panting. I remember her nude at the window and the lovely seed helicopters blowing in as she turned and showed me her ample front on purpose. That was my most romantic moment. Now for that kind of thing it's the degradation of Larney's Consenting Adult Viewing Center. Before it started getting to me, I'd bring bootloads of quarters and a special bottom cushion and watch hours and hours of Scandinavian women romping. It was shameful. Finally last Christmas I said enough is enough, I'd rather be sexless than evil. And since then I have been. Sexless and good, but very very tense. Since then I've tried to live above the fray. I've tried to minimize my physical aspects and be a selfless force for good. When mocked, which is nearly every day, I recall Christ covered with spittle. When filled with lust, I remember Gandhi purposely sleeping next to a sexy teen to test himself. After work I go home, watch a little TV, maybe say a rosary or two.

Thirty more years of this and I'm out of it without hurting anybody or embarrassing myself.

on **SOPHIE'S CHOICE**   WILLIAM STYRON

Tongue. Getting tongue, giving tongue. Sucking face. Frenching, French-kissing (but no French Lick, mind you, except in Indiana). As I oft say, I couldn't be a bigger fan of kissing, but I've never been much for frenching, even in France (where, as with their similarly miss-appelled fry, it seems not to be their forte). Something about the wriggliness of tongues moving in mouths other than their own reminds me of irked and predatory morays leering out of coral embankments. A tiny bit of tongue is okay, but it should never jut, nor dig, nor probe, nor slip along the teeth. All these are, to me, exceedingly vulgar and detract from the sublime nobility of kissing— lips mashed, heads pressed together, preferably with the dishwasher girl in the alley behind the motor oil drums...

I realize my one-tongue-in-my-mouth-at-a-time maximum is not commonly accepted. Many people seem to like lingual interloping— how many times have I had to flee just-crumpled sheets to escape oral excavation, my uvula battered and scraped and set to scab and peel later in little gag-inducing flakes? *Quelle horreur!* The French should have kept their reprehensible practices on their own shores. If only people would stick to what I call eskimo frenching, that delicate, back and forth, glottal *pas de deux* that allows the tongue to actualize itself fully as a refined instrument, the tool of the trade of such varied aesthetes as Paul Prudhomme and Dizzy Gillespie. But no, the unWaterpik-ed throng insists on all their prodding and poking, driving tongue-points toward the larynx like atavism-crazed lemmings. Pity.

And thus it is with no small amount of trepidation that I present the following excerpt, a conspicuous blight in an otherwise, by turns, delightful and harrowing masterpiece, William Styron's *Sophie's Choice*. Though many people find it sexy, I pray, dear reader, that you do not. If you do, seek help.

94 //

from William Styron's SOPHIE'S CHOICE

Side by side we gazed at the landscape. In the shadows her face was so close to mine that I could smell the sweet ropy fragrance of the sherry she had been drinking, and then her tongue was in my mouth. In all truth I had not invited this prodigy of a tongue; turning, I had merely wished to look at her face, expecting only that the expression of aesthetic delight I might find there would correspond to what I knew was my own. But I did not even catch a glimpse of her face, so instantaneous and urgent was that tongue. Plunged like some writhing sea-shape into my gaping maw, it all but overpowered my sense as it sought some unreachable terminus near my uvula; it wiggled, it pulsated, and made contortive sweeps of my mouth's vault: I'm certain that at least once it turned upside down. Dolphin-slippery, less wet than rather deliciously mucilaginous and tasting of Amontillado, it had the power in itself to force me, or somehow get me back, against a doorjamb, where I lolled helpless with my eyes clenched shut, in a trance of tongue. How long this went on I do not know but when at last it occurred to me to reciprocate or try to, and began to unlimber my own tongue with a gargling sound, I felt hers retract like a deflated bladder, and she pulled her mouth away from mine, then pressed her face against my cheek. "We can't just now," she said in an agitated tone. I thought I could feel her shudder, but I was certain only that she was breathing heavily, and I held her tightly in my arms. I murmured, "God, Leslie...Les"—it was all I could summon—and then she broke apart from me. The grin she was now grinning seemed a little inappropriate to our turbulent emotion, and her voice took on a soft, light-hearted, even trifling quality, which nonetheless, by force of its meaning, left me close to an insanity of desire. It was the familiar tune but piped this time on an even sweeter reed. "Fucking," she said, her whisper barely audible as she gazed at me, "fantastic...fucking." Then she turned and went back toward the living room.

on "THE BALLAD OF THE LONELY MASTURBATOR" ANNE SEXTON

The literature of masturbation consists, predominately, of sto-ries of boys wanking away, killing time during that phase when there's little else they are able to do with any compe-tency. Having dutifully perused our Roth and Bellow, contemporary read-ers are if anything a bit over-informed about the superhuman feats pimply males may achieve and the range of vessels they find appropriate for their seed. Having aged considerably from those days of delirium, however, I'm now more interested in what masturbation means for adults. For self-loving doesn't necessarily become easier as we amass experience. What starts as an activity filled with shame becomes shame-ful for different reasons. I think that by the time we become adults we make peace with the fact that we are sexual beings who need outlets. But, in my case at least, that youthful shame has been replaced by the feeling that I should have found my life partner by now, should have traipsed over the threshold and into connubial bliss and not still be wak-ing up alone and needy. As I get older, masturbation advertises itself as a kind of booby prize, not a natural element of the human sexual makeup, but evidence of just how sad and unfinished my still-single life is.

I am sure it needn't feel this way. Masturbation is healthy, we all know that, and it no doubt remains healthy from the exploratory tickles of infancy to the compensatory touches of age. Masturbation for adults should be, as Woody Allen put it, sex with someone we love. And yet, the very act frames us in such intense solitude that, feeling ourselves that much alone, we can't always access the love we have for the self. While masturbation at its best reminds us of our self-sufficiency, our libido, our ability to create joy for ourselves, at its worst it underscores whatever alienation, loneliness, incompleteness and self-hatred we retain from our less formed years. To borrow some words from Eliot, desire in this case might be rather over-mixed with memory.

Which brings us to the poem below by Anne Sexton. I first came to know her work through her diverse, sexy, heavy-hitting love poems. From among these, I want to put forth one that is more bitter than sweet—Sexton's take on adult self-pleasuring. Sexton's poem reveals that no matter how much Betty Dodson has done to teach us all to please ourselves, the demons continue to haunt, the past doesn't vanish and we enter our summer years still unshielded from the pains of echoing solitude.

Anne Sexton's
"THE BALLAD OF THE LONELY MASTURBATOR"

The end of the affair is always death.
She's my workshop. Slippery eye,
out of the tribe of myself my breath
finds you gone. I horrify
those who stand by. I am fed.
At night, alone, I marry the bed.

Finger to finger, now she's mine.
She's not too far. She's my encounter.
I beat her like a bell. I recline
in the bower where you used to mount her.
You borrowed me on the flowered spread.
At night, alone, I marry the bed.

Take for instance this night, my love,
that every single couple puts together
with a joint overturning, beneath, above,
the abundant two on sponge and feather,
kneeling and pushing, head to head.
At night, alone, I marry the bed.

I break out of my body this way,
an annoying miracle. Could I
put the dream market on display?

I am spread out. I crucify.
My little plum is what you said.
At night, alone, I marry the bed.
Then my black-eyed rival came.
The lady of water, rising on the beach,
a piano at her fingertips, shame
on her lips and a flute's speech.
And I was the knock-kneed broom instead.
At night, alone, I marry the bed.
She took you the way a woman takes
a bargain dress off the rack
and I broke the way a stone breaks.
I give back your books and fishing tack.
Today's paper says that you are wed.
At night, alone, I marry the bed.
The boys and girls are one tonight.
They unbutton blouses. They unzip flies.
They take off shoes. They turn off the light.
The glimmering creatures are full of lies.
They are eating each other. They are overfed.
At night, alone, I marry the bed.

on THE VENETIAN EPIGRAMS

JOHANN WOLFGANG VON GOETHE

Viva Italia, indeed. If not for the pasta, the olive oil, the architecture, the wines, the beaches, the Vespas, the fashion, the gelato, the Vatican, the footwear, the pleasant demeanor of the general populace and the dazzling superabundance of dark-eyed beauties, one could certainly love Italy for the language and the effect it's had on world literature. It's an interesting irony that Italy's foremost writer, Dante, was exiled much of his life, while many of the premier writers from the rest of Europe spent time in *il bel paese* and developed their writerly personas there. Chaucer and Milton both cut their literary teeth soon after (or during) extended trips to Italy; Byron too got much of his inspiration during his travels (carting along with him a small monkey!); and Goethe, jewel of Germany, made a number of trips south, composing some of his finest verse in or about Venice and Rome.

Goethe's Roman elegies are elegant, ethereal love poems; the Venetian cousins, meanwhile, are scathing, scabrous send-ups—wonderful little eyeholes to the dark side of the Meister. They're not sweet, but they are short, so I'm going to reprint four, to give a sense of their range. In the first, Goethe is picked up by two Venetian women; when he resists their advances, they know he's not from Venice. In the second, he adapts the scurrilous story from Rabelais of Hans Carvel putting the wrong "finger" in the "ring"; in the third, he laments his need to use the German language to write about the penis; and in the fourth, he explains why he prefers girls to boys (in words that will remind you of Sade). So while Goethe might be internationally famous for his immortal *Faust* or his exquisite, gentle, *The Sorrows of Young Werther*, we shouldn't forget his naughty side, which seems to have found a *petite Mort à Venice*.

from Johann Wolfgang von Goethe's VENETIAN EPIGRAMS

37

"Are you a foreigner, sir? Do you live in Venice?"
Two "lizards" asked me who'd lured me into their cave.
Guess!—"You're French! Neapolitan!" They bantered
Back and forth, meanwhile swiftly sipping their coffee.
"Let's do something!" said the loveliest, setting her cup
Down, and at once I felt her rummaging hand.
Gently I grasped and held it; the second one stretched
Forward her delicate fingers; I restrained them too.
"Ah, he's a foreigner!" both of them cried; they jested,
Asked me for presents which I, though sparingly, gave.
Thereafter they offered me a more secluded retreat
And the later hours of night for a warmer game.
If these creatures at once knew a stranger through signs of
        resistance,
O therefore you know why the Venetian creeps wanly about.

41

Expensive rings I own: engraved, precious gems
Of handsome design and style mounted in pure gold.
A person pays dearly for rings set with fiery stones;
Often you've seen them shine at the gaming table.
But I know a little ring that is excellent in another way—
The one old Hans Carvel once in his sadness possessed.
Unwisely he placed the smallest of his ten fingers
Into it; only the largest, the eleventh, belonged there.

38

Give me not "tail" but another word, o Priapus,
For, being a German I'm evilly plagued as a poet.
I call you phallos in Greek, which rings well in the ears;

And mentula's Latin, which can also serve as a word.
Mentula may come from mens, the tail's something behind,
And I never as yet had very much fun from that quarter.

40

I'm fairly fond of boys, but my preference is girls;
When I have enough of a girl, she serves me still as a boy.

on HERCULINE BARBIN: BEING THE RECENTLY DISCOVERED MEMOIRS OF A NINETEENTH-CENTURY FRENCH HERMAPHRODITE

If you want to open a restaurant, you should do it quickly. Times are a-changing, and it's going to be very difficult to keep up with the new building codes. Just think about bathrooms. Now that gender and sexual identity are no longer functions of the genitalia you were born with, it's clear that the old two-bathroom situation is not going to cut it. By my count, businesses starting up in the near future will need no fewer than twelve separate loos. The placards on the doors will probably read something like:

Straight Women

Straight Men

Gay Women

Gay Men

Neither

Both

Men in Women's Bodies

Women in Men's Bodies

Halfway M to F

Halfway F to M

Undecided

Fielder's Choice

In cities like Tokyo and New York where space is tight, this will prevent the development of most new buildings. Rents will skyrocket. Construction costs will go through the roof. Better get grandfathered in while you can.

This excerpt is taken from a manuscript that the celebrated French theorist Michel Foucault claimed to have discovered: the nineteenth-century diary/memoir of Herculine Barbin, born a hermaphrodite, raised in a convent as a girl, only to be judged a man by the French court when she was in her late twenties. Foucault was right to ask: "Do we truly need a true sex?" Herculine Barbin would have fared better in a world less bent on establishing her/his gender. We are not yet that world, but we are moving closer.

from HERCULINE BARBIN: BEING THE RECENTLY DISCOVERED MEMOIRS OF A NINETEENTH-CENTURY FRENCH HERMAPHRODITE

Once the prayers had been said and the students were in bed, we would often chat for hours at length, my friend and I. I would go and visit her at her bed, and it was my happiness to give her those little attentions that a mother gives her child. Bit by bit I got into the habit of undressing her. She had only to take out a pin without my help, and I would be almost jealous! These details will seem trivial no doubt, but they are necessary.

When I had laid her upon her bed, I would kneel beside her, my forehead brushing her own. Her eyes would soon close beneath my kisses. She had gone to sleep. I would gaze at her lovingly, unable to find the strength to tear myself away from her. I would awaken her. "Camille," she would say to me then, "I beg you, go to sleep. You will be cold, and it is late."

Finally overcome by her pleas, I would go gently away, but not before I had hugged her repeatedly against my breast. What I felt for Sara was not friendship; it was real passion.

I didn't love her. I adored her!

These scenes were re-enacted every day.

Often I would wake up in the middle of the night. Then I would slip stealthily up to my friend, promising myself that I would not disturb her angelic sleep; but could I contemplate that sweet face without drawing my lips close to it?

Consequently, after a restless night, I would have difficulty waking up when the morning bell rang. Always ready first, Sara would come to my bed to give me a parting kiss!

She would hurry the lingerers, say the prayer and then attend to combing the students' hair. I would help her in this task, but, alas! I did not have her skill, her delicate touch, and so the children would be careful to keep themselves as far away from me as they could.

When this chore was over, everyone would finish dressing. During that time, I would go with Sara to say good morning to Madame P. It was with the greatest joy that the excellent woman saw the intimacy that prevailed between her daughter and myself, and she rewarded us for it with a thousand affections. She kept for us as surprises all the things we liked to eat.

Sometimes it was a fruit, the first picked in her garden; sometimes it was a delicacy of the kind she excelled in making!

A little before eight o'clock Sara would go up to the dormitory to take off her dressing gown and put on other clothing. I did not allow her to do it without me. We were alone then. I would lace her up; with an unspeakable happiness I would smooth the graceful curls of her naturally wavy hair, pressing my lips now upon her neck, now upon her beautiful naked breast!

Poor dear child! How often did I cause a blush of astonishment and shame to rise to her brow! While her hand drew my own aside, she fixed her clear eyes upon me in order to fathom the reason for behavior that seemed to her the height of folly, and must have been.

—TRANSLATED BY RICHARD MCDOUGALL

on THE CONFESSIONS OF
JEAN-JACQUES ROUSSEAU

Who would expect one of the eighteenth-century's preeminent philosophers to have been a flasher? But then, in the
gamut of sex crimes, flashing is down there with the most
innocent—not so much a Jeffrey Dahmer–level activity as somewhere
between Benny Hill and Bambi. Flashing is a light, almost friendly sex
crime. So I suppose the next time I have to gape at somebody's goods
in Central Park, instead of calling for the cops I should simply respond
to my assailant: Well, isn't that nice.

Our good associations with flashing have not been lost on
Madison Avenue. Take the late-1980s poster campaign for the promo-
tion of museum-going: "Expose Yourself to Art." It depicted a middle-
aged man flashing a statue of a woman. Very amusing, but more
amusing is the fact that the guy in the photo later went on to become
the mayor of Portland, Oregon. And Europeans think we're prudish
about sex and politicians!

Even so, the future mayor of Portland is one thing, a canonized
mainstay of Philosophy 101 is another. But Rousseau's *Confessions*
pulls no punches, touching on all the flounderings and failings of young
J.J.'s life. Like Augustine before him, who even admitted to enjoying
sucking his mother's nipple, Rousseau puts all his dirty laundry out to
view—and makes an intensely human document in the process. He's a
charmer and a character, and even when he's flashing the neighborhood girls, our sympathies are with him. And just think: alchemists
searched long and hard for the philosopher's stone; if you were in the
right place near the end of the eighteenth century, you might have had
a chance to see both of Rousseau's.

from THE CONFESSIONS OF JEAN-JACQUES ROUSSEAU

I was a restless dreamer, my mind muddled. As I wept and sighed, I longed for a happiness I couldn't imagine, but nonetheless still wanted. It is impossible to describe this state; very few people would even be able to imagine it, because so few of them have experienced this fullness of life, at once both tormenting and delicious, which, in the intoxication of desire, suggest the foretaste of enjoyment. My hot blood kept my brain continually filled with images of girls and women; but, still not knowing about the relations of sex, I could only use them in my imagination in a manner consonant with my distorted ideas, without knowing what else to do; and these ideas kept my feelings in a state of most uncomfortable agitation; nor, thankfully, did I know how to deliver myself . . . Shame, the companion of a bad conscience, had appeared with my advancing years; it had increased my natural shyness to such an extent that it seemed insurmountable; and never, neither then nor later, could I bring myself to make an indecent proposal, unless the woman to whom I made it, had, to some extent, led me to it with her forwardness. . . .

My agitation had increased to such an extent that, being unable to satisfy my desires, I excited them by performing the most outrageous acts. I took to haunting dark alleys and secret retreats, where I might be able to expose myself to women, displaying to them the state that I would have liked to have achieved in their company. I didn't consider what I showed them obscene; I never thought of it that way. I thought it was merely ridiculous. The absurd pleasure I took in displaying it before their eyes cannot be described.

—TRANSLATED BY JACK MURNIGHAN

on GRAVITY'S RAINBOW   THOMAS PYNCHON

𝔍t's a writer's worst nightmare: you've assembled the cast of your novel for an orgy, and now you've got to write it. It's hard enough trying to describe one sex act, let alone ten. Simultaneously. Yes, narrating team hanky-panky ain't easy: name too many characters, acts or positions in a row and it reads like a grocery list; try to keep upping the sexiness level and you slide quickly into the absurd. Orgy scenes make every writer wish he or she were a photographer. Assemble the bodies, click, you're done. But to get it in words, as my Little Italy neighbors would say: fuggedaboutit.

That said, there are a few brave souls who have tried their best, and in this case it comes from an unlikely source, Thomas Pynchon's epic *Gravity's Rainbow*. In the first volume of *Naughty Bits*, I excerpted *Gravity's Rainbow*'s scandalous coprophagy scene; here we get another round of Pynchon's envelope-pushing, as we step aboard the good ship *Anubis* for some aristocratic saturnalia.

If you don't remember the pages in question, don't fret; Pynchon's 1973 masterwork is so enormous that, even if you managed to finish it, it's easy to forget just how lewd its lewd parts are. Though considered one of the great American writers since the war, Pynchon is not above the occasional deep purple prose. When the protagonist Slothrop gets hauled up the gunwales of the *Anubis* (and us with him), the seabound revelers are already chanting their call to arms—each other's. ("Welcome aboard, gee, it's a fabulous or-gy / That you just dropped in on, my friend / We can't recall how it star-ted, / But there's only one way it can end!") Soon the spanking of a princess sets off the erotic powder keg. It's bonafide smut from a master novelist, but it reads a bit more comically than Pynchon probably intended. Clear evidence that it's as hard to pull off a good orgy in fiction as it is in life.

from Thomas Pynchon's **GRAVITY'S RAINBOW**

"Oh, delightful," cries the meat-cleaver lady, "Greta's going to punish her."

"How I'd like to," murmurs a striking mulatto in a strapless
gown, pushing forward to watch, tapping Slothrop's cheek with her
jeweled cigarette holder as satin haunches whisper across his thigh.
Someone has provided Margherita with a steel ruler and an ebony
Empire chair. She drags Bianca across her lap, pushing up frock and
petticoats, yanking down white lace knickers. Beautiful little girl buttocks rise like moons. The tender crevice tightens and relaxes, sus-
pender straps shift and stretch as Bianca kicks her legs and silk
stockings squeak together, erotic and audible now that the group has
fallen silent and found the medium of touch, hands reaching out to
breasts and crotches, Adam's apples bobbing, tongues licking
lips...where's the old masochist and monument Slothrop knew
back in Berlin? It's as if Greta is now releasing all the pain she's
stored over the past weeks onto her child's naked bottom, the skin so
finely grained that white centimeter markings and numerals are
being left in mirror image against the red stripes with each blow,
crisscrossing building up a skew matrix of pain on Bianca's flesh.
Tears go streaming down her inverted and reddening face, mixing
with mascara, dripping onto the pale lizard surfaces of her mother's
shoes...her hair has loosened and spills to the deck, dark, salted with
the string of little pearl seeds. The mulatto girl has backed up against
Slothrop, reaching behind to fondle his erection, which has nothing
between it and the outside but someone's loosely pleated tuxedo
trousers. Everyone is kind of aroused, Thanatz is sitting up on the
bar having his own as yet unsheathed penis mouthed by one of the
white-gloved Wends. Two of the waiters kneel on deck lapping at
the juicy genitals of a blonde in a wine velvet frock, who meantime is
licking ardently the tall and shiny French heels of an elderly lady in
lemon organza busy fastening felt-lined silver manacles to the wrists
of her escort, a major in the Yugoslav artillery in dress uniform, who

kneels with nose and tongue well between the bruised buttocks of a long legged ballerina from Paris, holding up her silk skirt for him with docile fingertips while her companion, a tall Swiss divorcee in tight leather corselette and black Russian boots, undoes the top of her friend's gown and skillfully begins to lash at her bare breasts with the stems of half a dozen roses, red as the beads of blood which spring up and are soon shaking off the ends of her stiff nipples to splash into the eager mouth of another Wend who's being jerked off by a retired Dutch banker sitting on the deck, shoes and socks having just been removed by two adorable schoolgirls, twin sisters in fact, in identical dresses of flowered voile, with each of the bankers big toes inserted now into a downy little furrow as they lie forward along his legs kissing his shaggy stomach, pretty twin bottoms arched to receive in their anal openings the cocks of the two waiters who have but lately been, if you recall, eating that juicy blonde in that velvet dress back down the Oder River a ways...

on "THE DEBAUCHEE"

JOHN WILMOT, EARL OF ROCHESTER

One of the undiluted joys of my life has been to wake in the arms of my lover, slide myself atop her, make luscious morning love, watch her get up, dress and leave for work, then roll back over and sleep till noon. There is no richer sleep than the ante meridiem postcoital, knowing that, while you saw log after oneiric log, your one and only is nine-to-fiving on your behalf.

I was lucky enough to savor this joy every now and then for much of my twenties. By a series of curious quirks of fate, I held jobs from the ages of ten to twenty (first as a busboy in my stepfather's restaurant, then as a dishwasher in a Chinese Mafia front), but was more or less unemployed from twenty to thirty. For most of that period, I was either living the bohemian good life in Europe on money I had saved, or doing a Ph.D. and reading on my back all day. I had discovered the life of leisure, and I liked it.

Eventually adulthood caught up with me, and I was forced back to work. Now, like most people, I set a morning alarm, pack my lunch in Tupperware and come home after dark. My beloved sleeps beside me, then sends me off with a kiss. Ironically, now that I've found someone with whom I can make the most of loving and being in love, I have the least time to do so. This morning, after one snooze too many, I tried to sneak over her sleeping torso to drag on my pants and run to the office. She lolled awake, not knowing the time, and pulled me close. There were doves outside the window and I couldn't hear the clock . . .

This poem is a celebration of sloth, of sex and of sleeping late. It's by that naughty seventeenth-century rake John Wilmot, earl of Rochester. Though the early bird might catch the worm, the late bird, ah, the late bird . . .

John Wilmot, earl of Rochester's **"THE DEBAUCHEE"**

I rise at eleven, I dine about two,
I get drunk before sev'n; and the next thing I do,
I send for my whore, when for fear of a clap,
I spend in her hand, and I spew in her lap;
Then we quarrel and scold, 'till I fall fast asleep,
When the bitch, growing bold, to my pocket does creep;
Then slyly she leaves me, and, to revenge the affront,
At once she bereaves me of money and cunt.
If by chance then I wake, hotheaded and drunk,
What a coil do I make for the loss of my punk?
I storm and I roar, and I fall in a rage,
And missing my whore, I bugger my page.
Then, crop-sick all morning, I rail at my men,
And in bed I lie yawning 'till eleven again.

on FOREVER...   JUDY BLUME

One often hears people lamenting the fact that primary and secondary school teachers are underpaid and under-respected compared to their university counterparts. The argument is persuasive: grade school and high school teachers are reaching kids at the most dynamic stages in their developmental process, thus the education and example they give has the greatest impact, for better or worse. So why not require more training for schoolteachers than for professors, and why not give them at least an equal dose of money and prestige? In the trucking industry, drivers who carry fragile, volatile or dangerous materials make considerably more than their stable load–carrying peers; education should be the same way, and anyone who has worked closely with nitroglyceral teenagers knows what I'm talking about. A few of my college professors made some kind of impact on my life, but they had it easy; I was knocking on the door of adulthood by the time I made their acquaintance, and I came looking to learn. Whereas the two early teachers who helped make me who I am today had a lot to overcome: my seventh-grade teacher, who would throw candy to any of us who could point out the gerunds in a *New York Times* article; and my senior English teacher, who taught the AP students that literature is a vehicle for ideas, not for plots, and helped us to understand how beautiful those ideas could be. Unlike the impatient placeholders who are more interested in teaching discipline than understanding, great teachers do what no professor can ever do: bring the wisdom of age to people who are hell-bent on reject-ing the adult world.

The same can be said of writers in the Young Adult genre, who struggle, like high school teachers, to be given the respect they deserve. Yet their impact can hardly be overstated. For one example, there's a whole generation of young women who learned about sex from the pages of Judy Blume. Even as a boy growing up in the Midwest, I got some sex tips, or at least some arousal, reading *Then Again, Maybe I Won't*. (Thinking back now, I would always read it by flashlight in my closet!) But while most parents would probably be more comfortable seeing their young Janie reading Young Adult novels than something like *Nerve*, Blume is famous for infusing her tender teen tales with a lot of raunch. Blume's work in sex education through fiction was singularly progressive for the time, though there are a number of ideas that girls might have been better off without. The passage below, from her famous *Forever...*, is a case in point. Boys naming their dicks? Anything you do feels good? Not what I'd teach in Men 101. (In fact, whenever I get asked now if my dick has a name, I say: "You mean, the Führer?") But even if we were to tinker with some of the particulars, Blume was pointing us in the right direction. So here it is, just back from Memory Lane, the most dog-eared scene from what might well be the most popular—and influential—teen sex handbook in America.

from Judy Blume's FOREVER...

I got into bed and waited. In a few minutes Michael opened my door. He was wearing his same blue pajamas. He kind of waved at me and said "Hi."

"Hi," I answered.

He put his glasses on the night table, turned out the light and climbed into bed beside me. After we'd kissed for awhile he took off his pajama top, then said, "Let's take yours off too... it's in the way."

I slipped my nightgown over my head and dropped it to the floor. Then there were just my bikini pants and Michael's pajama bottoms between us. We kissed again. Feeling him against me that way made me so excited I couldn't lie still. He rolled over on top of me and we moved together again and again and it felt so good I didn't ever want to stop—until I came.

After a minute I reached for Michael's hand. "Show me what to do," I said.

"Do whatever you want."

"Help me Michael...I feel so stupid."

"Don't," he said, wiggling out of his pajama bottoms. He led my hand to his penis. "Katherine...I'd like you to meet Ralph... Ralph, this is Katherine. She's a very good friend of mine."

"Does every penis have a name?"

"I can only speak for my own."

In books penises are always described as hot and throbbing but Ralph felt like ordinary skin. Just his shape was different—that and the fact that he wasn't smooth, exactly—as if there was a lot going on under the skin. I don't know why I'd been so nervous about touching Michael. Once I got over being scared I let my hands go everywhere. I wanted to feel every part of him.

While I was experimenting, I asked, "Is this right?"

And Michael whispered, "Everything's right."

When I kissed his face it was all sweaty and his eyes were half closed. He took my hand and led it back to Ralph, showed me how to hold him, moving my hand up and down according to his rhythm. Soon Michael moaned and I felt him come—a pulsating feeling, a throbbing, like the books said—then the wetness. Some of it got on my hand but I didn't let go of Ralph.

We were both quiet for a while, then Michael reached for the tissue box by the side of the bed. He passed it to me. "Here...I didn't mean to get you."

"That's all right...I don't mind..." I pulled out some tissues.

He took the box back. "I'm glad," he said, wiping up his stomach.

I kissed the mole on the side of his face. "Did I do okay...considering my lack of experience?"

He laughed, then just put his arms around me. "You did just fine...Ralph liked it a lot."

on THE RIG VEDA

Before the dawn of civilization, sex must have been a pretty dicey affair. Looking at comparables among our animal friends, it's hardly encouraging. There is one species of ape (the Bonobo) that lives in a sex-crazed matriarchal utopia, and I've been told there's a kind of female lizard that gets pregnant without any help from the male (why leave the house?), but other than these, the wild kingdom doesn't seem to provide many examples of sex being better for creatures lacking language and neurosis.

The urge to mate is often figuratively called an itch, but early man probably felt the itch in a much more literal sense. The need to reproduce, like a mosquito bite, was there, he attended to it and that was it—drop to the ground, stick it in, jerk it twice, stand up, pull the mastodon skins back up and resume berry picking.

I'd like to believe that civilization, even in its crudest form, probably improved things a bit. As the quest for food and water became more organized and predictable, leisure time must have emerged in all its glory. Suddenly, what was previously done simply for survival could be explored for its potential for pleasure. This is not to suggest that early man gave up raw flesh and immediately discovered chateau briand with bernaise, but maybe there were a few members of *Homo Aestheticus* who had and took the time to learn to shag with style. (Ironically, men's discovery of the clitoris might well have coincided with the advent of irrigated farming...)

In any case, by the time the Egyptians were drawing pictograms on leaves and the Sumerians were figuring out how to scratch characters into clay, sex was clearly a serious business, and women were hoping for more than a simple wham, bam. Vases from all around the Mediterranean show that cultures in the millennia before Christ were quite familiar with the wide world of whoopie, employing as many positions as you or I are likely to and bringing a variety of adult aids into play, including cock rings and love lotions. In a sense, it stands to reason that early stages in human development could have facilitated the best sex in history: we were civilized enough to have spare time, but had no TV or Condensed Classics to compete for our attention. If you've got a decent amount of time on your hands and there's nothing else to do but screw, you're likely to get pretty good at it.

My theory is borne out by the earliest works of literature. The oldest book in the Indo-European tradition, the Sanskrit *Rig Veda* of circa 1,000 B.C. (that's right kids, three centuries before Homer and Hesiod), is positively chock-full of nookie. More than a dozen of its thousand-plus poems concern both wives and husbands trying to get their partners to have sex with them, and there is a near-constant innuendo in the imagery of many of the rest. In the poem below, the god Indra's wife, Indrani, is complaining because Indra's friend (and perhaps son), Vrsakapi, is trying to bed her. Indra doesn't seem too worried about it, though, and even invited Vrsakapi back to his house in the end (for a seeming orgy). What a happy resolution!

from THE RIG VEDA

INDRANI: They no longer press the Soma, nor do they think of Indra as God, now that my friend Vrsakapi has gorged himself on the nourishments of the enemy. Indra supreme above them all!

Indra, you pass over the erring ways of Vrsakapi. No, you will not find Soma to drink in any other place. Indra supreme above them all!

INDRA: What has this tawny animal, this Vrsakapi, done to you that you are so jealous of him, and begrudge him the nourishing wealth of the enemy? Indra supreme above all!

INDRANI: The ape has defiled the precious, well-made, anointed things that are mine. I will cut off his "head," and I will not be good to that evil-doer. Indra supreme above all!

No woman has finer loins than I, or is better at making love. No woman thrusts against a man better than I, or raises and spreads her thighs more. Indra supreme above all!

VRSAKAPI: O little mother, so easily won, as it will surely be, my loins, my thigh, my "head" seem to thrill and stiffen, little mother. Indra supreme above all!

INDRA: Your arms and fingers are so lovely, your hair so long, your buttocks so broad. You are the wife of a hero—so why do you attack our Vrsakapi? Indra supreme above all!

INDRANI: This imposter has set his sights on me as if I had no man. But I have a real man, for I am the wife of Indra, and the Maruts are my friends. Indra supreme above all!

VRSAKAPI: In the past, this lady would go to the public festival or to a meeting-place. There she would be praised as one who sets all in order, the wife of Indra, a woman with a man. Indra supreme above all!

WIFE OF VRSAKAPI: Indrani is the most fortunate among women, I have heard, for her husband will never die of old age. Indra supreme above all!

VRSAKAPI: Wife of Vrsakapi, you are rich in wealth and in good sons in your son's wives. Let Indra eat your bulls and the oblation that is so pleasing and so powerful in effect. Indra supreme above all!

WIFE OF VRSAKAPI: Like a sharp-horned bull bellowing among the herds of cows, a mixture is being prepared for you, Indra, that will please your heart and refresh you. Indra supreme above all!

INDRANI: That one is not powerful, whose penis hangs between his thighs; that one is powerful for whom the women's hairy organ opens as the penis swells and sets to work. Indra supreme above all!

INDRA: How many miles separate the desert and the ploughed land! Come home, Vrsakapi, and we two will meet in agreement, so that you who destroy sleep may come again on the homeward path. Indra supreme above all!

THE POET: As you went home to the north, Vrsakapi, where was the beast of many sins? To whom, O Indra, did the inciter of people go? Indra supreme above all!

The daughter of Manu, name Parsu, brought forth twenty children at once. Great happiness came to her whose womb felt the pains. Indra supreme above all!

—TRANSLATED BY WENDY DONIGER O'FLAHERTY

on THE RAVISHING OF LOL STEIN

MARGUERITE DURAS

Conventional wisdom would have us believe that the more emotionally deep characters in a novel are, the more poignant the reading experience will be. Toni Morrison's *Beloved* is a perfect example: because of the staggering emotional richness of its dramatis personae, it gets me (and almost everyone else) all swollen-eyed with every read. Morrison's characters emote across an incredibly broad spectrum, and we roller-coast right alongside them.

Marguerite Duras's early novel *The Ravishing of Lol Stein* provides an interesting counterpoint. If you come to *Lol Stein* having only read Duras's *The Lover*, you're in for quite a shock. *Lol Stein* is a study in emotional detachment, in the disaffection we sometimes think plagues modern life. But reading *Lol* indicates just how far we are from real emotional distance—the title character's detachment is so creepy, so alienating, you feel like you've been rubbing elbows with a vampire. There have been times in my life when I suspected I might be a robot, but next to Lol Stein, even my most muted emotional responses look positively operatic.

In this scene, Lol is alone with Jack Hold, the novel's narrator, her lover and the lover of her best friend and rival, Tatiana Karl. By this point in the novel, Lol's libido is expressed almost exclusively through acts of passive voyeurism. She wants to be the spurned lover, the third wheel—she doesn't engage in any other way. Hold is fascinated by her, ready to leave Tatiana for her, but that isn't what Lol wants. She is only interested in him because she has seen him with Tatiana. Lol's is a kind of madness, brought on by extreme suffering, where the world has become something she can only witness. And thus she, like the reader, gazes in from the outside. But we, unlike her, feel the events as they transpire.

"The woman who arrived on the square where all the buses meet was Tatiana Karl."

I don't answer her.

"It was Tatiana. You're a man who sooner or later was bound to be drawn to her. I knew that."

Her eyelids are covered with fine droplets of perspiration. I kiss her closed eyes, they move beneath my lips, her eyes are hidden. I let her go. I leave her. I move to the opposite end of the room. She remains where she is. I want to find out something...

"The light went on in your room, and I saw Tatiana walk in front of the light. She was naked beneath her black hair."

She does not move, her eyes staring out into the garden, waiting. She has just said that Tatiana was naked beneath her dark hair. That sentence is the last to have been uttered. I hear: "naked beneath her dark hair, naked, naked, dark hair." The last two words especially strike with a strange and equal intensity. It's true that Tatiana was as Lol has just described her, naked beneath her dark hair. She was that way in the locked room, for her lover. The intensity of the sentence suddenly increases, the air around it has been rent, the sentence explodes, it blows the meaning apart. I hear it with a deafening roar, and I fail to understand it, I no longer even understand that it means nothing.

Lol is still far from me, rooted to the floor, still turned toward the garden, unblinking.

The nudity of Tatiana, already naked, intensifies into an overexposed image which makes it increasingly impossible to make any sense whatsoever out of it.

The void is statue. The pedestal is there: the sentence. The void is Tatiana naked beneath her dark hair, the fact. It is transformed, poured out lavishly, the fact no longer contains the fact, Tatiana emerges from herself, spills through the open windows out over the town, the road, mire, liquid, tide of nudity. Here she is, Tatiana Karl, suddenly naked beneath her hair, between Lol Stein and me. The sentence has just faded away, I can no longer hear any sound, only silence, the sentence is dead at Lol's feet, Tatiana is back in her place. I reach out and touch, like a blind man I touch and fail to recognize anything I have already touched. Lol is waiting for me to recognize something, not that I be attuned to her vision but that I no longer be afraid of Tatiana. I am no longer afraid. There are two of us now, beholding Tatiana naked beneath her dark hair. Blindly, I say:

"An extraordinary lay, Tatiana."

There was a movement of her head. Lol's tone is one I have never heard from her before, shrill and plaintive. The wild animal removed from its forest home sleeps, dreams of the equator of its birth, trembles in its sleep, its dream of sunlight, weeps.

"The best, the best one of them all, right?"

I say:

"The best."

I go to Lol Stein. I kiss her, lick her, breathe in the odor that is Lol, kiss her teeth. She does not move. She has grown beautiful. She says:

"What an amazing coincidence."

I do not reply. Again I leave her, standing there far from me, in the middle of the living room. She does not even seem to realize that I have moved away from her. Again I say:

"I'm going to leave Tatiana Karl."

—TRANSLATED BY RICHARD SEAVER

As information technology improves, certain sectors of the human brain seem to weaken. Memory is one: while most of us have a hard time remembering whether there's milk in the fridge, six centuries before the birth of Christ, rhapsodes in Greece (like Plato's Ion) could recite all of Homer's *Iliad* and *Odyssey* by heart. The ability to compose music seems to be another: as much as I like the tunes of the last hundred years, even the record companies would have to admit that they are the least sublime since the Dark Ages. Finally, I've heard it argued that our poetic capacities are on the wane—or perhaps our use of language as a whole. It's quite possible that technology isn't to blame for these changes; they might be symptoms of larger cultural dynamics, of which technology might itself only be a component. But, in any case, it is clear there are few if any poetic cultures in the modern world, and the poetry that's being written is held in less and less esteem. Weep on, sisters of the sacred well.

If it is true that the world today is at a kind of low point in its dedication to poetry, what points in history have been the highest? Certain cultures have produced multiple poetic geniuses within the same generation (Britain's brief but lustrous Romantic period is a conspicuous example), but no nation, to my mind, can be as proud of its early poetic history as Japan. Beginning in the seventh century, the ability to generate extemporaneous poems of the highest quality was an integral part of being esteemed in the Japanese court. These days, I get a lot of mileage at cocktail parties by generating spontaneous limericks to order, but even my best attempts would have had me laughed out of Kyoto. Japanese court poems, though often only thirty-one syllables long, are marvels of small packaging—they are ornate vials that often contain the grandest of themes distilled to a rich infusion.

No surprise, then, that although Lady Murasaki's eleventh-century *Tale of Genji* is sometimes considered the first novel in the history of world literature, I enjoy it more for its verse achievements than its prose narrative. In the course of its eleven hundred pages, Genji and his cohorts swap over eight hundred crafted couplets and allude to hundreds more. In the scene below, the exchange of poems between Genji and the old crone, Naishi, who is trying to seduce him, retell the narrative line in a kind of soft, exquisite obligato. If there is an art to doublespeak and innuendo, this is it.

from Shikibu Murasaki's THE TALE OF GENJI

There was a lady of rather advanced years called Naishi. She was wellborn, talented, cultivated and widely respected; but in matters of the heart she was not very discriminating. Genji had struck up relations, interested that her wanton ways should be so perdurable, and was taken somewhat aback at the warm welcome he received. He continued to be interested all the same and had arranged a rendezvous. Not wanting the world to see him as the boy lover of an aged lady, he had turned away further invitations. She was of course resentful.

One morning when she had finished dressing the emperor's hair and the emperor had withdrawn to change clothes, she found herself alone with Genji. She was bedecked and painted to allure, every detail urging him forward. Genji was dubious of this superannuated coquetry, but curious to see what she would do next. He tugged at her apron. She turned around, a gaudy fan hiding her face, a sidelong glance—alas, the eyelids were dark and muddy—emerging from above it. Her hair, which of course the fan could not hide, was rough and stringy. A very poorly chosen fan for an old lady, he thought, giving her his and taking it from her. So bright a red that his own face, he was sure, must be red from the reflection, it was decorated with a gold painting of a tall grove. In a corner, in a hand that was old-fashioned but not displeasingly so, was a line of poetry: *"Withered is the grass of Oaraki."* Of all the poems she could have chosen!

"What you mean, I am sure, is that *your grove is summer lodging for the cuckoo.*"

They talked for a time. Genji was nervous lest they be seen, but Naishi was unperturbed.

"Sere and withered though these grasses be
They are ready for your pony, should you come."

She was really too aggressive.

"Were mine to part the low bamboo at your grove,
It would fear to be driven away by other ponies
And that would not do at all."

He started to leave, but she caught at his sleeve. "No one has ever been so rude to me, no one. At my age I might expect a little courtesy."

These angry tears, he might have said, did not become an old lady.

"I will write. You have been on my mind a great deal." He tried to shake her off but she followed after...

The ladies of the palace were beginning to talk of the affair-a most surprising one, they said. To no Chujo heard of it. He had thought his own affairs varied, but the possibility of a liaison with an old woman had not occurred to him. An inexhaustibly amorous old woman might be rather fun. He arranged his own rendezvous. He too was very handsome, and Naishi thought him not at all poor consolation for the loss of Genji. Yet (one finds it hard to condone such greed) Genji was the one she really wanted . . .

[One evening Genji] came up to her door. She joined in as he sang: "Open my door and come in." Few women would have been so bold.

"No one waits in the rain at my eastern cottage.
Wet are the sleeves of the one who waits within."

It did not seem right, he thought, that he should be the victim of such reproaches. Had she not yet, after all these years, learned patience?

> "*On closer terms with the eaves of your eastern cottage*
> *I would not be, for someone is there before me.*" ...

To no Chujo had been on the watch for an opportunity to give his friend a little of what he deserved. Now it had come. The sanctimonious one would now be taught a lesson.

It was late, and a chilly wind had come up. Genji had dozed off, it seemed. To no Chujo slipped into the room. Too nervous to have more than dozed off, Genji heard him, but did not suspect who it would be. The superintendent of palace repairs, he guessed, was still visiting her. Not for the world would he have had the old man catch him in the company of the old woman.

"This is a fine thing. I'm going. *The spider surely told you to expect him, and you didn't tell me.*"

He hastily gathered his clothes and hid behind a screen. Fighting back laughter, To no Chujo gave the screen an unnecessarily loud thump and folded it back. . . Still ignorant of the latter's identity, Genji thought of headlong flight; but then he thought of his own retreating figure, robes in disorder, cap all askew. Silently and wrathfully, To no Chujo was brandishing a long sword.

"Please, sir, please."

Naishi knelt before him wringing her hands. He could hardly control the urge to laugh. Her youthful smartness had taken a great deal of contriving, but she was after all nearly sixty. She was ridiculous, hopping back and forth between two handsome young men. To no Chujo was playing his role too energetically. Genji guessed who he was. He guessed too that this fury had to do with the fact that he was himself known. It all seemed very stupid and very funny. He gave the arm wielding the sword a stout pinch and To no Chujo finally surrendered to laughter.

"You are insane," said Genji. "And these jokes of yours are dangerous. Let me have my clothes, if you will."

But To no Chujo refused to surrender them.

"Well, then, let's be undressed together." Genji undid his friend's belt and sought to pull off his clothes, and as they disputed the matter Genji burst a seam in an underrobe.

"Your fickle name so wants to be known to the world
That it bursts its way through this warmly disputed garment.

"It is not your wish, I am sure, that all the world should notice."

Genji replied:

"You taunt me, sir, with being a spectacle
When you know full well that your own summer robes are showy."

Somewhat rumpled, they went off together, the best of friends. But as Genji went to bed he felt that he had been the loser, caught in such a very compromising position.

An outraged Naishi came the next morning to return a belt and a pair of trousers. She handed Genji a note:

"I need not comment now upon my feelings.
The waves that came in together went out together,
leaving a dry river bed."

—TRANSLATED BY EDWARD G. SEIDENSTICKER

on SMALL WORLD

DAVID LODGE

All my life I've been haunted by the phrase "Once an *x*, always an *x*." It started when I left the Midwest of my birth and rearing and went Out East for college: I spent years trying to hide my Illinois accent and knowledge of nitrogen cycles and fit in with all the Ivy League kids. But once a Midwesterner, always a Midwesterner, as I would soon find out—on the squash court among other places. Around the same time I also tried to make the uncomfortable switch from being a "math person" to being a "book person." Jesus, all those pages, all those character names and nicknames—I thought I'd never keep the Buendía family or the Karamazov brothers straight.

Eventually I did succeed in becoming a book person and went on to get a Ph.D., only then to leave the academy and try my way in the all-too-real world. The big question, of course, was whether I could shake off my academic trappings, stop quoting Spenser at dinner parties and learn to leave the bow ties in the closet. It was a painful lesson to realize that it didn't behoove me to flip through Latin flash cards while waiting in line at a club, nor to smoke a pipe at a rock concert. So I adapted, slowly. For some of us, it's hard to be young, and I learned how only after my youth had faded.

But the fact is, even though I am now decked out in the same hipster duds that all the kids are wearing, and often write for those new-fangled dot com things (whatever that means), I am still a geek and always will be. It's my nature, through and through. So I take great joy (and experience very little guilt) going back and re-reading David Lodge's lighthearted academic send-ups, *Small World* and *Changing Places*. One of Lodge's characters is modeled on an old professor of mine, resulting, for me, in a strange collapsing of past and present, fiction and fact. It's a small world indeed, and Lodge's warmth and humor help keep it spinning.

I was sitting opposite Joy. She was wearing a soft blue velour dressing gown with a hood, and a zip that went from hem to throat . . . Joy was, I guessed, in her early thirties, with fair wavy hair and blue eyes. A rather heavy chin, but with a wide, generous mouth, full lips. She had a trace of a northern accent, Yorkshire I thought. She did a little English teaching, conversation classes at the university, but basically saw her role as supporting her husband's career. I daresay she made the effort to get up and be hospitable to me for his sake. Well, as we talked, and ate, and drank, I suddenly felt myself overcome with the most powerful desire for Joy.

It was as if, having passed through the shadow of death, I had suddenly recovered an appetite for life that I thought I had lost forever, since returning from America to England. In a way it was keener than anything I had ever known before. The food pierced me with its exquisite flavours, the tea was fragrant as ambrosia, and the woman sitting opposite to me seemed unbearably beautiful, all the more because she was totally unconscious of her attractions for me. Her hair was tousled and her face was pale and puffy from sleep, and she had no makeup or lipstick on, of course. She sat quietly, cradling her mug of tea in both hands, not saying much, smiling faintly at her husband's jokes, as if she'd heard them before. I honestly think that I would have felt just the same about any woman, in that situation, at that moment, who wasn't downright ugly. Joy just represented woman for me then. She was like Milton's Eve, Adam's dream—he woke and found it true, as Keats says. I suddenly thought how nice women were. How soft and kind. How lovely it would be, how natural, to go across and put my arms round her, to bury my head in her lap. All this while Simpson was telling me about the appalling standards of English-language teaching in Italian secondary schools. Eventually he glanced at his watch and said that it had gone four, and instead of going back to bed he thought he would drive to Milan while he was wide awake and rest when he got there. He was taking the Council car, he told me, so Joy would run me to the airport in theirs.

He had his bag already packed, so it was only a few minutes before he was gone. We shook hands, and he wished me better luck with my flight the next day. Joy went with him to the front door of the apartment, and I heard them kiss goodbye. She came back into the living room, looking a little shy. The blue dressing gown was a couple of inches too long for her, and she had to hold up the skirt in front of her—it gave her a courtly, vaguely medieval air as she came back into the room. I noticed that her feet were bare. "I'm sure you'd like to get some sleep now," she said. "There is a second bed in Gerard's room, but if I put you in there he might be scared when he wakes up in the morning." I said the sofa would be fine. "But Gerard gets up frightfully early, I'm afraid he'll disturb you," she said. "If you don't mind taking our bed, I could quite easily go into his room myself." I said no, no; she pressed me and said would I just give her a few moments to change the sheets, and I said I wouldn't dream of putting her to such trouble. The thought of that bed, still warm from her body, was too much for me. I started to shake all over with the effort to stop myself from taking an irrevocable leap into moral space, pulling on the zip tab at her throat like a parachute ripcord, and falling with her to the floor.

Anyway, there we were looking at each other. We heard a car accelerate away outside, down the hill, Simpson presumably. "What's the matter?" she said, "You're trembling all over." She was trembling herself a little. I said I supposed it was shock. Delayed reaction. She gave me some more brandy, and swallowed some herself. I could tell that she knew it wasn't really shock that was making me tremble, that it was herself, her proximity, but she couldn't quite credit her own intuition. "You'd better lie down," she said, "I'll show you the bedroom."

I followed her into the main bedroom. It was lit by a single bedside lamp with a purple shade. There was a large double bed with a duvet half thrown back. She straightened it out and plumped the pillows. I was still shaking all over. She asked me if I would like a hot water bottle. I said, "There's only one thing that would stop me shaking like this. If you would put your arms round me..."

Although it was a dim light in the room, I could see that she went very red. "I can't do that," she said. "You shouldn't ask me."

"Please," I said, and took a step towards.

Ninety-nine women out of a hundred would have walked straight out of the room, perhaps slapped my face. But Joy just stood there. I stepped up close to her and put my arms round her. God, it was wonderful. I could feel the warmth of her breasts coming through the velour dressing gown and my shirt. She put her arms round me and gently clasped my back. I stopped shaking as if by magic. I had my chin on her shoulder and I was moaning and raving into her ear about how wonderful and generous and beautiful she was, and what ecstasy it was to hold her in my arms, and how I felt reconnected to the earth and the life force and all kinds of romantic nonsense. And all the time I was looking at myself reflected in the dressing-table mirror, in this weird purple light, my chin on her shoulder, my hands moving over her back, as if I were watching a film or looking into a crystal ball. It didn't seem possible that it was really happening. I saw my hands slide down the small of her back and cup her buttocks, bunching the skirt of her dressing gown, and I said to the man in the mirror, silently, in my head, you're crazy, now she'll break away, slap your face, scream for help. But she didn't. I saw her back arch and felt her press against me. I swayed, and staggered slightly, and as I recovered my balance I altered my position a little, and now in the mirror I could see her face, reflected in another mirror on the other side of the room, and, my God, there was an expression of total abandonment on it, her eyes were half shut and her lips were parted and she was smiling. Smiling! So I pulled back my head and kissed her, full on the lips. Her tongue went straight into my mouth like a warm eel. I pulled gently at the zip on the front of her dressing gown and slid my hand inside. She was naked underneath it.

I slipped the dressing gown from her shoulders, and it crackled with static electricity as it slid off and settled at her feet. I fell on my knees and buried my face in her belly. She ran her fingers through my hair, and dug her nails into my shoulders. I lay her down on the bed and began to tear off my clothes with one hand while I kept stroking her with the other, afraid that if I once let go of her, I would lose her. I had just enough presence of mind to ask if she was protected, and she nodded, without opening her eyes. Then we made love. There was nothing particularly subtle or prolonged about it, but I've never had an orgasm like it, before or since. I felt I was defying death, fucking my way out of the grave. She had to put her hand over my mouth, to stop me from shouting her name aloud: Joy, Joy, Joy.

Okay, someone, please tell me what men are thinking. Why is the idea of a woman giving a blowjob to a horse exciting? This I just don't get. A woman is a woman, and a horse, as far as I can tell, is just a horse. Yes, they have big horsey members, which, I suppose, might make them appealing to women. But why is this appealing to men? It seems almost like saying, I would love to have sex with you, darling, but I'd be even more turned on if you had sex with the four-hundred-pound football player who lives next door. (Which, now that I think about it, some men do like...)

Could it be that a woman being with a horse (or a dog, for that matter) somehow indicates, in the minds of the men watching, the depth of her need for penises? Or that this woman really wants sex—unlike all those women with whom the consumers of such material strike out regularly. Are these guys thinking, "Wow, if she'll suck off Secretariat, my chances must be pretty good," or is the idea that she could want that much, that badly, erotically appealing in itself?

My guess is that some kind of transference must be taking place. I remember the first time I saw a porn movie—it was surprisingly late in life, I think near the end of high school. The movie was a Marilyn Chambers vehicle, and I was very impressed that the filmmakers had created story lines where incredibly average-looking, average-seeming guys get to have sex with the lovely Marilyn. The dumpy pool man, the shaggy cable guy, etc. I somehow thought this was a technique discrete to her films: make the viewer identify with the guys in the narrative so his fantasy of actually being able to have a threeway with Chambers and her busty cousin from out of town becomes imaginable—even possible. Hey, if I ended up cleaning the pool of the right woman...

It didn't take me long to find that a lot of porn is based on this principle—thus explaining, for any women still wondering, why the men in porn are traditionally so mediocre looking. If the guy boffing Jenna Jameson happened to be hot, that would suggest that in porn, as in life, ordinary schmos don't get to have sex with nymphomaniacal bombshells.

Identification is clearly vital to porn working properly. So why, then, the horses? What's there for the average porn viewer to see of himself? Well, the average leading horse is a hairy, sweaty, priapic, emotionally indifferent mammal with a two-digit IQ. Ring any bells?

from John Irving's THE CIDER HOUSE RULES

"Come look at this, Sunshine," Melony said. She was trying to pick the tack loose with her fingernail, but the tack had been stuck there for years. Homer knelt beside Melony on the rotting mattress. It took awhile for him to grasp the content of the photograph; possibly, he was distracted by his awareness that he had not been as physically close to Melony since he'd last been tied to her in the three-legged race.

Once Homer had understood the photograph (at least, he understood its subject, if not its reason for existing), he found it a difficult photograph to go on looking at, especially with Melony so close to him. On the other hand, he suspected he would be accused of cowardice if he looked away. The photograph reflected the cute revisions of reality engineered in many photographic studios at the turn of the century; the picture was edged with fake clouds, with a funereal or reverential mist; the participants in the photograph appeared to be performing their curious act in a very stylish Heaven or Hell.

Homer Wells guessed it was Hell. The participants in the photograph were a leggy young woman and a short pony. The naked woman lay with her long legs spread-eagled on a rug—a wildly confused Persian or Oriental (Homer Wells didn't know the difference)—and the pony, facing the wrong way, straddled her. His head was bent, as if to drink or graze, just above the woman's extensive patch of pubic hair; the pony's expression was slightly camera-conscious, or ashamed, or possibly just stupid. The pony's penis looked longer and thicker than Homer Well's arm, yet the athletic-looking young woman had contorted her neck and had sufficient strength in her arms and hands to bend the pony's penis to her mouth. Her cheeks were puffed out, as if she'd held her breath too long; her eyes bulged; yet the woman's expression remained ambiguous—it was impossible to tell if she was going to burst out laughing or if she was choking to death on the pony's penis. As for the pony, his shaggy face was full of faked indifference—the placid pose of strained animal dignity.

"Lucky pony, huh, Sunshine?" Melony asked him, but Homer Wells felt passing through his limbs a shudder that coincided exactly with his sudden vision of the photographer, the evil manipulator of the woman, the pony, the clouds of Heaven or the smoke of Hell. The mists of nowhere on this earth, at least, Homer imagined. Homer saw, briefly, as fast as a tremble, the darkroom genius who had created this spectacle. What lingered with Homer longer was his vision of the man who had slept on this mattress where he now knelt with Melony in worship of the man's treasure. This was the picture some woodsman had chosen to wake up with, the portrait of pony and woman somehow substituting itself for the man's family. This was what caused Homer the sharpest pain; to imagine the tired man in the bunkroom at St. Cloud's, drawn to this woman and this pony because he knew of no friendlier image—no baby pictures, no mother, no father, no wife, no lover, no brother, no friend.

But in spite of the pain it caused him, Homer Wells found himself unable to turn away from the photograph. With a surprisingly girlish delicacy, Melony was still picking at the rusty tack—in such a considerate way that she never blocked Homer's view of the picture.

"If I can get the damn thing off the wall," she said, "I'll give it to you."

"I don't want it," said Homer Wells, but he wasn't sure.

"Sure you do," Melony said. "There's nothing in it for me. I'm not interested in ponies... You get it, don't you, Sunshine?" she asked Homer Wells. "You see what the woman's doing to the pony, right?"

"Right," said Homer Wells.

"How'd you like me to do to you what that woman is doing to that pony?"

There be three things which
are too wonderful for me,
yea, four which I know not:
The way of an eagle in the air;
the way of a serpent upon a rock;
the way of a ship in the midst of the sea;
and the way of a man with a maid.
— Proverbs 30

𝕴 have known the joys of seduction, I have known the thrill of the
chase, the simultaneous empowerment and disempowerment
of pursuit, of feeling you might but not yet feeling you will. I,
like Saint Augustine, have felt more strongly about that which was
harder to attain, and I, like Job, have felt that I was unfairly tested, and,
in my frustration, asked only to be delivered. I have desired and been
spurned, only later to be embraced, and I have relished that turn-
around, that surprise. I have enjoyed kisses from people I thought I had
lost, gone on dates with those I thought impossible. Once I was
engaged to a woman I never would have believed could want me, only
to realize, one day, the truth that I didn't want her. I have known people
who dream and are rarely disappointed and those for whom disappointment has taught them never to dream again. I am neither of these
people; I dream, and I fail, and it hurts me, so when I succeed I feel the
force of the success, the brief, rapturous sense that maybe I deserve my
achievement, however fleeting it may be.

There was a time when my ego needed the reinforcement that
seduction provides, yet no amount of conquest ever proved enough.
The seducer assumes that the quest is for something external, but it is
clear that the lack comes from within. How much affirmation does one

need? And from whom? I was told once by a policeman in India that happiness is a quotient of what you have divided by what you want. In the West, he told me, you try to increase the numerator, accumulating more and more of everything. In the East, he said, they try to reduce the denominator, trimming their expectations to correspond to what's probable. I think he had it dead on, and what's worse, as the numerator increases—as we begin to get what we thought we were after—it often causes us to set our aims higher and not reap the rewards of what we've achieved.

Serial seduction, like gambling, is all too likely to fall prey to this dynamic. Each conquest ups the ante for the subsequent one, and that which is desired, when attained, loses its value. A sad phenomenon, more so because the objects in question are emotive humans. The perils of sexual insatiability are chronicled in two great fictional studies: Laclos's *Dangerous Liaisons* and Kierkegaard's *Diary of the Seducer*. Now I'm excerpting two paragraphs of the latter to indicate the poles of the seducer's logic: the attraction that makes him grab and the repulsion that makes him throw away. A word to the wise...

from Søren Kierkegaard's DIARY OF THE SEDUCER

My eyes can never become tired of hastening over this peripheral manifoldness, these scattered emanations of womanly beauty... Each one has her own; the cheerful smile, the roguish glance, the desiring eye, the inclined head, the hilarious mind, the quiet wistfulness, the profound foreboding, the brooding melancholy, the earthly homesickness, the unrepentant movements, the beckoning brow, the questioning lips, the mysterious brow, the captivating locks, the concealing eyelashes, the heavenly pride, the earthly modesty, the angelic purity, the clandestine blush, the light step, the lovely gliding, the languishing posture, the yearning dream, and unexplained sighs, the slim figure, the soft forms, the luxuriant bosom, the swelling hips, the little foot, the pretty hand. Each one has her own, and the one does not have what the other has. When I have seen and seen again, considered and again considered the manifoldness of the world, when I have smiled, sighed, flattered, threatened, desired, tempted, laughed, cried, hoped, feared, won, lost... then the passion flares up. This one girl, the only one in the whole world, she must belong to me, she must be mine...

I am an aesthete, an eroticist, who has grasped the essence of love and the point of it, who believes in love and knows it from the ground, and only retain for myself the private opinion that every love affair should, at the most, last six months, and that every relationship is over as soon as one has enjoyed the ultimate. I know all this, I know also that the highest conceivable enjoyment consists in being loved; to be loved is higher than everything in the world. To poetize oneself into a girl's feelings is an art, to poetize oneself out of her feelings is a masterpiece. But the latter essentially depends on the former.

—TRANSLATED BY GEORGE L. STENGREN

In one of his short stories, Borges writes that the desert is the perfect labyrinth. Nothing is as inescapable and relentless as the vast iteration of its monotony. The desert's emptiness forms the backdrop for Paul Bowles's *The Sheltering Sky* and the erotics of the anonymous, the blank, the tabula rasa onto which one can inscribe one's own fantasy. In one scene, a blind prostitute shimmers like an oasis for the male protagonist, Port—a promise of something he's convinced himself he needs. Yet as the book progresses, it becomes clear that the desert is less a metaphor for the desire of Port's heart as much as for the emptiness of his heart itself.

After his untimely death, his wife Kit is forced to go on the run in the middle of the Sahara, without the benefit of knowing Arabic. Her escape initiates Bowles's second parable of the erotics of anonymity; she takes up with a traveling caravan, and must trade her body for her passage with the caravan leaders with whom she cannot speak.

Here Bowles does what few male writers are bold enough to do: write a scene of nonconsensual sex from the woman's perspective. Nor does he stop there: he takes the risk of having her enjoy it. Not immediately, as you will see, but eventually Kit is transformed by the hands of the stranger in the strange land. And here again the desert insinuates itself as Bowles's primary metaphor. Her lover, Belqassim, is himself, like Port's blind dancer, an analog of the desert. Escaping into it, she escapes into him. But more than that, it becomes clear that Bowles is showing both sides of the same coin; the desert is an enormous amphitheater in which characters can confront the ineluctable mystery of themselves. This is what passes for love in *The Sheltering Sky*: anonymity and inscrutability as a screen for the dumbshow of the self. Elegant, sexy and serene as the staging is, let us hope not to be caught in such labyrinths ourselves.

Presently the older man stood at the side of the rug, motioning to her to get up. She obeyed, followed him across the sand a short way to a slight depression behind a clump of young palms. There Belqassim was seated, a dark form in the center of a white rug, facing the side of the sky where it was apparent that the moon would shortly rise. He reached out and took hold of her skirt, pulling her quickly down beside him. Before she could attempt to rise again she was caught in his embrace. "No, no, no!" she cried as her head was tilted backward and the stars rushed across the black space above. But he was there all around her, more powerful by far; she could make no movement not prompted by his will. At first she was stiff, gasping angrily, grimly trying to fight him, although the battle went on wholly inside her. Then she realized her helplessness and accepted it. Straightway she was conscious only of his lips and the breath coming from between them, sweet and fresh as a spring morning in childhood. There was an animal-like quality in the firmness with which he held her, affectionate, sensuous, wholly irrational—gentle but of a determination that only death could gainsay. She was alone in a vast and unrecognizable world, but alone only for a moment; then she understood that this friendly carnal presence was there with her. Little by little she found herself considering him with affection: everything he did, all his overpowering little attentions were for her. In his behavior there was a perfect balance between gentleness and violence that gave her particular delight. The moon came up, but she did not see it.

on THE HISTORY OF MY MISFORTUNES

PETER ABELARD

Т he way it's normally told, it's as sad a love story as Romeo and Juliet's: Peter Abelard, the foremost philosopher of twelfth-century Europe, has a secret love affair with a brilliant young girl named Heloise, until one day her father finds out, has his servants castrate Abelard and sends Heloise to a nunnery, never to see Abelard again. From that point on, they exchange letters on the poignancy of their love for each other and their sadness at each other's absence. This is the way you normally hear about them, but the facts of the matter are a bit different. Abelard was castrated, but Heloise had already been sent to the convent to hide from her father the fact that she was pregnant. And though she wrote Abelard, he didn't answer her for over twenty years, and when he did, his letters were emotionally glacial and chastisingly pious. He claimed that their sufferings were God's retribution for their sexual sins (including boffing in the convent's refectory) and more or less told her that his love for her had been replaced by his love for God. Ouch.

Heloise, however, remained steadfast. That's why I'm in love with her—or one of the reasons. It's not that I believe she should have stayed true to Abelard after so much neglect—the twelfth was quite a progressive century, after all—it's more that her letters display a level of passion, maturity and understanding that I find fantastically compelling. It is clear that Heloise had perspective both on herself and on the personal and psychological factors that motivated Abelard's silence. And she forgave him—that's why I love her. She was able to see all of his frailty, all his emotional weakness, and feel for him just the same. I empathize with Abelard's inability to act responsibly, I can even understand his aggressive religious defense in the face of his own shame. Many of us are unready for true love when it falls into our laps, and, until we can develop our hearts, we can only hope for a Heloise to forgive our trespasses.

Unfortunately, in Heloise's letters we get few details of her initial seduction. In Abelard's we do. He tells the story in his *History of My Misfortunes*, a letter ostensibly written to a friend but clearly intended for a larger audience. It eventually made its way to Heloise, prompting her to write Abelard again, and initiating the exchange of letters that is their famous correspondence. It's a paradigmatic tale of mind versus body: the smartest man seeks out the smartest woman, and, finding her, ends up in such a rhapsody of the flesh as to give up the mind entirely. Isn't that how it should be?

from Peter Abelard's THE HISTORY OF MY MISFORTUNES

There was in Paris at the time a young girl named Heloise, the niece of Fulbert, one of the canons, and so much loved by him that he had done everything in his power to advance her education in letters. In looks she did not rank lowest, while in the extent of her learning she stood supreme. A gift for letters is so rare in women that it added greatly to her charm and had won her renown throughout the realm. I considered all the usual attractions for a lover and decided she was the one to bring to my bed, confident that I should have an easy success; for at that time I had youth and exceptional good looks as well as my great reputation to recommend me, and feared no rebuff from any woman I might choose to honour with my love. Knowing the girl's knowledge and love of letters I thought she would be all the more ready to consent, and that even when separated we could enjoy each other's presence by exchange of written messages in which we could speak more openly than in person, and so need never lack the pleasures of conversation.

All on fire with desire for this girl I sought an opportunity of getting to know her through private daily meetings and so more easily winning her over; and with this end in view I came to an arrangement with her uncle, with the help of some of his friends, whereby he should take me into his house, which was very near my school, for whatever sum he liked to ask. As a pretext I said that my household cares were hindering my studies and the expense was more than I could afford. Fulbert dearly loved money and was moreover always ambitious to further his niece's education in letters, two weaknesses which made it easy for me to gain his consent and obtain my desire: he was all eagerness for my money and confident that his niece would profit from my teaching. This led him to make an urgent request which furthered my love and fell in with my wishes more than I had dared to hope; he gave me complete charge over the girl, so that I could devote all the leisure time left me by my school to teaching her by day and night, and if I found her idle I was to punish her severely. I was amazed by his simplicity—if he had entrusted a tender lamb to a ravening wolf it would not have surprised me more. In handing her over to me to punish as well as to teach, what else was he doing but giving me complete freedom to realize my desires, and providing an opportunity, even if I did not make use of it, for me to bend her to my will by threats and blows if persuasion failed? But there were two special reasons for his freedom from base suspicion: his love for his niece and my previous reputation for continence.

Need I say more? We were united, first under one roof, then in heart; and so with our lessons as a pretext we abandoned ourselves entirely to love. Her studies allowed us to withdraw in private, as love desired, and then with our books open before us, more words of love than of our reading passed between us, and more kissing than teaching. My hands strayed oftener to her bosom than to the pages; love drew our eyes to look on each other more than reading kept them on our texts. To avert suspicion I sometimes struck her, but these blows were prompted by love and tender feeling rather than anger and irritation, and were sweeter than any balm could be. In short, our desires left no stage of love-making untried, and if love could devise something new, we welcomed it. We entered on each joy the more eagerly for our previous inexperience, and were the less easily sated.

Now the more I was taken up with these pleasures, the less time I could give to philosophy and the less attention I paid to my school.

It was utterly boring for me to have to go to the school, and equally wearisome to remain there and to spend my days on study when my nights were sleepless with love-making. As my interest and concentration flagged, my lectures lacked all inspiration and were merely repetitive; I could do no more than repeat what had been said long ago, and when inspiration did come to me, it was for writing love-songs, not the secrets of philosophy.

—TRANSLATED BY BETTY RADICE

on STORY OF THE EYE   GEORGES BATAILLE

Since the eighteenth century, French philosophy has been in a decadent phase; clarity of presentation came to be less of a concern and precision of meaning lost out to drama and hyperbole. Philosophy became more like literature—not a bad thing, especially when seen against the bloodless Anglo-American model— and literature started to become a bit more like philosophy. Nowhere is this more evident than in the French pornographic tradition. Sade, Nin, Bataille, Réage—their achievements have few rivals in American erotica. What elevates these authors above other pornographic writers is their preoccupation with philosophy, their potent impulse to tease deep meanings from the grammar of what is called perversion.

The intersection of philosophy and pornography led, in French literature, to a great preoccupation with the nexus of sex and death. The import of sex moved beyond procreation, beyond recreation, becoming, in effect, the vehicle through which death infuses and inscribes itself within life (especially through orgasm, long referred to as "le petit mort"—the little death). Excrement plays a similar role, both in philosophy and eroticism: shit and piss are the death passed from the self. As such, they appeal to the ruminations of both philosophers and the most nihilistic of libertines.

French literary pornography interweaves all these threads, and Georges Bataille's first novel, *Story of the Eye*, is the supreme meditation. First published in France in the 1920s, it scandalized readers with the debauched misadventures of its teenaged protagonists who pee, fuck, frig and murder their way through France and Spain. As the novel progresses, they become increasingly obsessed with the symbolic, isomorphic overlap among eggs, eyes and testicles. Simone, the principal female, sits on eggs, pisses on eyes, and, discovering at a bullfight that the balls of a just-slain *toro* are also white and egg-shaped, veers toward madness. **The scene below enacts the philosophical layering that fascinates Bataille; it is spectacularly graphic, outlandish, unforgettable—and quintessentially French.**

from Georges Bataille's STORY OF THE EYE

It really was totally out of the question for Simone to lift her dress and place her bare behind in the dish of raw balls. All she could do was hold the dish in her lap. I told her I would like to fuck her again before Granero returned to fight the fourth bull, but she refused, and she sat there, keenly involved, despite everything, in the disembowelments of horses, followed, as she childishly put it, by "loss and noise," namely the cataract of bowels.

Little by little, the sun's radiance sucked us into an unreality that fitted our malaise—the wordless and powerless desire to explode and kick up our asses. We grimaced, because our eyes were blinded and because we were thirsty, our senses ruffled, and there was no possibility of quenching our desires. We three had managed to share in the morose dissolution that leaves no harmony between the various spasms of the body. We were so far gone that even Granero's return could not pull us out of that stupefying absorption. Besides, the bull opposite him was distrustful and seemed unresponsive; the combat went on just as drearily as before.

The events that followed were without transition or connection, not because they weren't actually related, but because my attention was so absent as to remain absolutely dissociated. In just a few seconds: first, Simone bit into one of the raw balls, to my dismay; then Granero advanced towards the bull, waving his scarlet cloth; finally, almost at once, Simone, with a blood-red face and a suffocating lewdness, uncovered her long white thighs up to her moist vulva, into which she slowly and surely fitted the second pale globule— Granero was thrown back by the bull and wedged against the balustrade; the horns struck the balustrade three times at full speed;

at the third blow, one horn plunged into the right eye and through the head. A shriek of unmeasured horror coincided with a brief orgasm for Simone, who was lifted up from the stone seat only to be flung back with a bleeding nose, under a blinding sun; men instantly rushed over to haul away Granero's body, the right eye dangling from the head.

——TRANSLATED BY PETER CONNOR

on PSYCHOPATHIA SEXUALIS

RICHARD VON KRAFFT-EBING

e lust for metaphors, us speakers. It's hard if not impossible to organize our thoughts, comprehend reality and communicate with others without using categories and analogies, all of which are metaphor-based. Nietzsche famously pointed out that no two leaves are the same, yet we hodgepodge them all into a single definition, give it a name and thus allow ourselves to talk about something that would otherwise be overly complex. Often these oversimplified categories get amplified beyond even their original meanings. Such is the case with *fetish*—first an anthropological term used to speak of the perceived irrationality of the idol-worship of "primitive" cultures, then a precise clinical word for an inanimate object that incites sexual arousal; it is now used loosely and metaphorically to speak of any excessive interest in or infatuation with something. In the popular press, the meaning of fetish has gotten so fuzzy and diffusely sexual that it now gets confused with or lumped in alongside sadomasochism, an entirely different psycho-sexual interest. There are now fetish clubs (usually S/M-centered), fetish gear (ditto) and fetish-fiction anthologies—these last containing truly heterogeneous stories, few involving fetish in the strict sense.

Among places to read of actual body and object fetishes, Richard von Krafft-Ebing's breakthrough turn-of-the-century *Psychopathia Sexualis* is particularly amusing. Compiling cases of sexual deviance (including such practices as bestiality, satyriasis, self-mortification and, shhh, homosexuality!), Krafft-Ebing says that "pathological fetishism is commonly a cause of psychic impotence." He goes on to explain that "it often happens that, due to his perversion, the fetishist diminishes his excitability to normal stimuli, or, at least, is capable of coitus only by concentrating his fantasy upon his fetish." To put it in a nutshell, if you need to stroke a high-heeled shoe to get an erection, you're a fetishist; if you like your girlfriend to wear leather boots, you're just normal.

On the winning side, Krafft-Ebing's accounts of grave-robbing necrophiliacs and small-penised neurasthenics are, by turns, macabre and comical. Unfortunately, his association of homosexuality with excessive masturbation is dated and embarrassing, as is his adherence to now-debunked theories of female hysteria. But overall, *Psychopathia Sexualis* makes for great reading, and gives an interesting overview of clinical psychology before Freud. Its great lesson? Beware the shrunken-headed masturbator!

from Richard von Krafft-Ebing's PSYCHOPATHIA SEXUALIS

Case 88

X., aged thirty-four, teacher in the high school. In childhood he suffered from convulsions. At the age of ten he began to masturbate, with lusty feelings, which were attached to most strange ideas. He was particularly fond of women's eyes, but because he wished to imagine some form of sexual relation, and was absolutely ignorant of the specifics of sexual matters, he developed the idea of making the nostrils the primary female sexual organs in order to avoid too great a distance from the eyes. His vivid sexual imagination then revolved around this idea. He sketched drawings representing accurate Greek profiles of female heads, but the nostrils were exaggerated to such an extent that insertion of the penis would have been possible.

One day, in a tram, he saw a girl in whom he thought his ideal was realized. He followed her to her home and immediately proposed to her. Shown the door, he returned time and again, until arrested. X. had never had sexual intercourse.

Nose fetishism is rarely encountered. The following obscure bit of poetry comes to me from England:

O sweet and pretty little nose, so charming unto me;
O were I but the sweetest rose, I'd give my scent to thee.
O make it full with honey sweet, that I may suck it all;
'Twould be for me the greatest treat, a real festival.
How sweet and how nutritious your darling nose does seem.
It would be more delicious, than strawberries and cream.

—TRANSLATED BY JACK MURNIGHAN

on "HOW TO RECOGNIZE A PORN MOVIE WHEN YOU SEE ONE"

UMBERTO ECO

Freudian psychotherapists make a big deal of kids seeing their parents screwing. Many a shrink, confronted with my battery of functionality-disabling neuroses, has asked if I ever snuck a peek. No way, man!—at least not that I remember. "Ja," they note, "not zat you remember. Very interestink." And then they write in their notebooks. Creepy, that writing-in-the-notebook thing, though they're probably just making grocery lists.

For me, the real concern is not seeing your parents having sex, but seeing yourself having sex. That's what's fucked up. As John Barth points out in his first novel, *The Floating Opera*, "If you are young and would live on love; if in the flights of intercourse you feel that you and your beloved are fit models for a Phidias, for a Michelangelo—then don't, I implore you, be so foolish as to include among the trappings of your love nest a good plate mirror. For a mirror can only reflect what it sees, and what it sees is screamingly funny." He's right, of course, it is funny—disastrously so, what with the (in my case) lily-white booty up in the air, the tongue a-loll, the arms and legs oh-so akimbo. Sex is a grim reminder that there are spectator sports and there are sports that are better just to play. Despite the success of porn as evidence to the contrary, it is clear that the beast with two backs does a most curious jig. To watch it successfully (pleasantly, that is), you have to divorce the act from the humans involved. The moment of peril comes when you recognize, Oh my god, that's ME! Yuck! To see copulation with anonymous or at least superhumanly famous participants allows enough anonymity for the indiscriminate sex button to be pushed (like the prostate G-spot that is supposed to make men come automatically), but to know the humans involved is to see sex non-symbolically, to reveal it as the atavistic twitch that it is.

Pornography is thus dependent on a certain distance from the everyday, while at the same time reliant on the illusion of realism (or at least the hint of possibility) that encourages the viewer to superimpose her- or himself over the protagonists. This need for mundane normalcy is the topic of one of Umberto Eco's hysterical "User's Manuals," short essays he wrote for an Italian magazine on everything from how to avoid infectious diseases to, in this case, how to recognize a porno movie. After reading this, you, like former Supreme Court Justice Stewart, will know porn when you see it.

from Umberto Eco's
"HOW TO RECOGNIZE A PORN MOVIE WHEN YOU SEE ONE"

I don't know if you've ever happened to see a porn movie. I don't mean movies with some erotic content, a movie like *Last Tango in Paris*, for example... No, what I mean is genuine porno flicks, whose true and sole aim is to stimulate the spectator's desire, from beginning to end, and in such a way that, other than the various and varied copulations, the rest of the story counts for less than nothing.

Magistrates often have to decide if a movie is purely pornographic or if it has some artistic merit... And, as it turns out, there is a criterion that can be used to decide; it is based on a calculation of time wasted... Porno movies, in order to justify the price of the ticket or videocassette, need to have certain people having sensual relations: men with women, men with men, women with women, women with dogs or horses. (I'll note in passing that there are no porno movies where men have sex with dogs or horses; why?) All of this would be fine, except they are full of wasted time.

If Gilbert, in order to rape Gilberta, has to go from the piazza at Cordusio to Buenos Aires, the film shows Gilbert driving, stoplight after stoplight, the length of the trip...

The reasons are obvious. A film in which Gilbert did nothing but rape Gilberta, from the front, from behind, from the side, wouldn't be sustainable, neither for the actors, nor economically for the producer. Nor would it be for the viewer: in order for transgression to work psychologically, it has to take place against a background of normalcy...

And thus porno movies are forced to represent everyday life, in a way that the viewer will recognize it. If Gilbert needs to take a bus from A to B, it shows Gilbert taking a bus from A to B.

This annoys the viewer, who would prefer if there were only scenes containing the unspeakable. But that's an illusion. One wouldn't be able to withstand an hour and a half of scenes of the unspeakable. The dead time is necessary...

And thus, I repeat: if you are in a movie theater, and the time it takes the protagonists to go from A to B is longer than what you would like it to be, then the film you are seeing is pornographic.

—TRANSLATED BY WILLIAM WEAVER,
MODIFIED BY JACK MURNIGHAN

on POEMS FROM THE SANSKRIT

When I was the editor of Nerve.com, I was often asked if I ever got tired of sex. I assume the people who asked were wondering about my job, wanting to know if I ever got sick of reading about sex, doing business about sex, writing about sex, and otherwise being steeped all the worklong day in sex. But despite all the subcomponents, their question came out plain and simple: Don't you ever get tired of sex? The answer, of course, is yes, I do get tired of sex, but that's why there's sleep and repose. A minimal dose of either tends to bring me around.

Tiring of sex in any other sense is hard to imagine, especially if you think not just of the procreative act, but of all the broad commerce between the potentially attracted. Sex, in the large sense, is that thing that makes me wake up in the morning, keeps me up at night, makes me walk, eat, think and breathe. I've lived more than thirty years on this earth's crust, and I can't say that I understand the motivations of other people. For me, the great bulk of human industry, when not directed toward finding, building or nurturing a great love, seems expendable. Philosophers are wont to look at the universe and ask why, but I, for one, have little doubt.

And thus sex, being the privileged vehicle toward arriving and communicating that love, is a logical *terminus ad quem* for most endeavors. It is the Rome all roads lead back to. Such is the sentiment of these probably fifth-century Sanskrit romantic poems, that nothing matters in this dumbshow but ladies with lotus eyes.

from POEMS FROM THE SANSKRIT

In this vain world, when men of intellect
Must soil their souls with service, to expect
A morsel at a worthless prince's gate,
How could they ever hope to renovate
Their spirits?—were it not that fate supplies
The swinging girdles and the lotus eyes —
Women, with swelling breasts that comfort soon,
Wearing the beauty of the rising moon.

—BHARTRHARI

Is she a pencil of ambrosia?
Is she a swelling flood of loveliness?
Is she the beauty of the lotus flower?
Is she a budding, flowering vine of love?
Now that I've seen this lovely, charming girl,
I cannot help but think that all the world,
Except for her, is utterly in vain.

—ANONYMOUS

In this vain fleeting universe, a man
Of wisdom has two courses: first, he can
Direct his time to pray, to save his soul,
And wallow in religion's nectar-bowl;
But, if he cannot, it is surely best
To touch and hold a lovely woman's breast,
And to caress her warm round hips, and thighs,
And to possess that which between them lies.

—BHARTRHARI

—TRANSLATED BY JOHN BROUGH

ou are a pervert. Or at least society tells you that you are. If acted upon, your sexual desires would take you outside the bounds of decorous behavior—and probably outside the law. All this you know too well. So what do you do? Therapy is expensive, inexact and often humiliating. Telling a perfect stranger that you dream about fucking teenage boys and murdering them afterwards, for example, is probably not an easy thing to do. Nor is shelling out ninety clams for forty-minute chat sessions five times a week. So what are your alternatives? Well, like anything in the world, you can either do it or you can write about it. The former route is likely to put more meals on your table (and get you a free black-and-white jumpsuit), but the latter is truer to the all-important distinction between thought and action. And therein lies the pull of much fantasy: the very fact that the images constructed will never be real, the dream never acted upon. Few critics of pornography manage to grasp this point: that, in some circumstances, it is the irreality of events portrayed that makes porn enticing. To use a simple example, I would never willingly treat a woman as badly as they are treated in some porn depictions, but it is nonetheless stimulating to imagine a sexual object that you have no ethical or personal concern for. This part of myself I can't deny. But I would never act on that stimulus; my sense of humanity and compassion would eliminate any pleasure that could be derived. And thus fantasy enters in, for in my imagination I can stage scenes and exploit their appeal, yet not victimize anyone directly. Fantasy scratches the amorality of our imaginations against the morality of our beliefs. The friction is its appeal.

All of this is good to keep in mind when reading Dennis Cooper novels. For the fuck and murder fantasy is common in his books in a variety of forms, yet you also detect a love and appreciation running through them (he reads like a sympathetic Bret Easton Ellis, if such a thing is imaginable). So when he told me that his novel *Guide* is his favorite, I considered excerpting some of its fantastic lines on ass-worship ("Junkies' asses are perfect, partly because they're so scrawny and, at the same time, being so constipated, such weird treasure chests"), or on young men ("You're like cream in the shape of a boy"), or on a dwarf porn star (no description necessary), but I decided on a scene that enacts the fantasy dynamic I've been describing in all its complexity. Cooper's protagonist, conveniently named Dennis, is trying to save a young HIV-positive junky/hustler who he's doing an article on for *Spin*. The kid's name is Sniffles, and, as it turns out, he likes to be smacked around, but at the same time he likes older men and wants a loving father figure. And thus the fantasy: of fulfilling both roles, of not forcing violence on the boy but having him ask for it, of weaving pain into an act of compassion in the same way that murder can be seen as a kind of deliverance. This is clearly the raw material of Cooper's libido, and unlikely to be realized. But it's also the stuff of which the contemporary novel is made.

from Dennis Cooper's GUIDE

Sniffles stares out the windshield for several minutes, watching neighborhoods change into other kinds of neighborhoods. I guess they're gentrifying the closer we get to my own. I never think about things like that. "So you're into kissing," he says without looking at me.

"I didn't say that."

Sniffles checks me out, his eyes charged with a thought that I'm far too excited about to begin to decode. "I don't know," he says. "That's sort of the one thing I'm really not into." Then he cringes, like he's sure I'll say no.

"How's about this," I say. "No kissing, but anything else is okay, and I'll give you . . . I don't know, five hundred dollars, if it's really amazing."

Sniffles's eyes freak. They practically electrocute me, the road ahead, his own crotch. "Shit, yeah," he shouts. "Whatever you want to do. That's...wow." He slides low in the seat, rests his Docs on the dashboard, and starts pounding out a rhythm on his knees. "Are you rich? Because you don't seem rich."

"No. I'm just spending *Spin*'s expense account."

"Great scam."

"I guess."

"So when you say 'amazing,' what do you mean?"

"Well, you're amazing."

He smiles cautiously. "I'm your type."

"Completely."

"That's cool," he says. He thinks for a second. "Yeah, that's really cool. I like you too. I have a thing for older guys. And I sort of like being told what to do. During sex, I mean, not in my life."

"Lucky me."

Sniffles studies my eyes. "So what's your thing? You want to fuck me without a condom? I mean, that's no problem, if you want to."

"No, no. God, you shouldn't do that."

"Yeah, I know." Sniffles grins. "Oh, I know what you're thinking."

"What?"

Sniffles stifles the grin, but it's still there, just stunted. "You want to hit me."

"Actually, I wasn't—" But now that he mentions it. Well, not "hit." That's not a word I would use. I might have said "rough." "Rough" sounds more...something.

"You can tell I'm into that, right?" Sniffles says. "Johns always know. They never even ask, they just start whaling on me."

I picture that scene for a few seconds. "Yeah, I could tell." Like Sniffles says, I'm weird.

"Wacky." He fixes his eyes on something far beyond the windshield. "I don't know why, but I love when guys hit me. I guess it's because of my dad or whatever. It's like my favorite fucking thing in the world."

"Lucky me," I say.

Sniffles's eyes search mine. "Cool, yeah. Listen, is there any possibility..." he says, smiling, "...that we could...have a relationship?"

"You mean, like boyfriends."

"Not the normal, boring kind of boyfriends. I mean, because I'm in love with David, you know? I just mean...not like a sugar daddy or anything. Maybe sort of like a father-figure type who'll beat the shit out of me when I'm feeling fucked up. That's sort of a huge fantasy."

"It's possible." I guess it is, although very remotely. Anyway, we're home. "That's the place." And I point.

overnment officials have always been more imaginative than fiction writers. The result is that real-life brutality is far more extreme than brutality in fiction. The most violent of novels—Cormac McCarthy's *Blood Meridian*, Sade's *120 Days of Sodom*, Bret Easton Ellis's *American Psycho*, or even the anonymous medieval *The Lay of Havelock the Dane*—seem tame alongside a year of Amnesty International reports. Psychological warfare is not dissimilar: though less visible, real human-to-human atrocities no doubt replicate and exceed all those we would find in literature. As far as fiction is able to plumb the thoughts and actions of characters, it is rare for writers to pursue the furthest limits of human behavior. Thankfully most of us never live through such extremes, so the practice of reading about them in books becomes that much more important.

Hal Bennett's underpraised novel *Lord of Dark Places* is just such an example. First page to last, Bennett's narrative manages to stay at pace with, if not outdistance, the most extreme of what we can imagine as possible. Set in the 1950s South, it is the story of Joe Market and his father Titus. After the twelve-year-old Joe watches Titus literally fuck his mother to death, they set off as a traveling religious sect, The Church of the Naked Disciple. Going from town to town, Titus evangelizes and then makes Joe strip off his clothes and, to the awe of the crowds, reveal his enormous tool. He is then pimped by Titus to support the "church" and Titus's own prostitute habit. What follows is the steady buildup of Joe's sexual identity—he comes to fancy himself as a terrestrial deity bearing the godhead between his legs—and its eventual demolition.

Bennett's novel of degradation, violence, incest and obsession is, by turns, both alarming and arousing. Its sex scenes are painted as forcefully as any I've read, and they're painted often. The scene below is not as explicit as some, but it shows the long-dormant sexuality of an older woman as it springs back to life in an act of desperate blackmail. Bennett's imagination, here as throughout his novel, is a hand torch in the deepest darkness.

from Hal Bennett's LORD OF DARK PLACES

Cheap Mary smacked her lips with heavy satisfaction. "I wasn't too sure about the facts, but I knew that you had killed that child. And for all these months now, I've been waiting in my kitchen window for you to come hopping back across that fence. I'm a patient woman, I knew that some day you'd come back. All things come back." She moved across the bed and pulled her dress above her wrinkled knees. "Now, there's a favor I want you to do for me. It's my price for keeping quiet. You do want me to keep quiet, don't you?"

He turned his head and looked at her thin legs with the blue veins imbedded in the freckled skin. "You want me to fuck you?" he said bluntly.

Cheap Mary shook her head. "Not that. I hate that. It hurts too much."

She kept her legs stretched out and pulled the dress a little higher up her thighs. He noticed for the first time that she wore high-buttoned shoes, the old-fashioned kind with high heels and pearl buttons studded in the gray suede material halfway up her leg...

"Then, you'll do me the favor?"

The idea of crawling between those mottled thighs disgusted him. He stripped the negligee and bloomers off and sat back on the bed...

He burst into tears. "Please don't make me do it."

Her eyes were full of pity, but he saw that she would not relent. "I need it, don't you understand? I'm going to die soon. It may be the last time before I die. Don't you have enough love in you for that, to satisfy another human being before she dies?"... She pulled her dress higher. "Do you suppose you could do me the favor? It's the only price I'm asking for my silence."

She reached out and clutched him firmly by the head. He was in a panic. How many times had he done the same thing to men and women, grabbing them by the head and tugging them with a slow, cruel smile into the nest of his sex? He resisted her pull, but desperation gave her strength, her fingers seemed made of wire.

"Come, dear child, you'll find it's not so unpleasant as it seems."

He held his breath. "That's right," Mary said, inching toward him, "that's right, just one more time before I die." Like ecstatic horns of Satan, the gray suede shoes dug into his butt.

on BOOK OF GOMORRAH: AN ELEVENTH-CENTURY TREATISE AGAINST CLERICAL HOMOSEXUAL PRACTICES Peter Damian

When a local paper reveals a new sex scandal involving a priest and a young boy, few people are surprised. The regularity of these scandals has rendered priestly pederasty almost a cliché. Sadly, the phenomenon is so common that it occludes the tragedy of each individual case. Making jokes about frocked sex offenders has the unfortunate effect of making pederasty more imaginable, while, at the same time, encouraging us to take its offenders less seriously. To that extent, at least, the publicity perpetuates the phenomenon more than stigmatizes it.

But perhaps the press coverage is more representative of our desire for scandal than of the actual predilections of some clergymen. The conventional logic, of course, is that priests, denied the release of sexual encounters, are left stewing in whatever desires they are unable to rid themselves of. And, clearly, if these desires are "unnatural" in the first place, then taking a vow of chastity would seem an attempt at further prohibiting them, of nipping them in the bud, if you will. In some cases this kind of preemption probably succeeds. In others it obviously does not, and the results are often more sordid than they would have been had the original desires been acted upon through conventional channels.

Regardless of whether priests are actually more inclined to pederasty than anyone else, the association is not new, as the excerpt below shows. Taken from an eleventh-century book-length invective against homosexuality among priests, the passage demonstrates that not only were homosexuality and pederasty common in the Middle Ages, but so little was being done about it that the author, Peter Damian, an Irishman, felt the need to speak out violently. His verbal assault is sweeping and relentless and, to the modern eye, somewhat comical. But despite his overblown rhetoric, Damian clearly believed that homosexuality and pederasty were the foremost faults with the medieval priesthood. Nine centuries of civilization have done little to erode the stereotype.

from Peter Damian's BOOK OF GOMORRAH: AN ELEVENTH-CENTURY TREATISE AGAINST CLERICAL HOMOSEXUAL PRACTICES

"A Mournful Lament for the Soul Who Is
Given over to the Filth of Impurity"

O, I weep for you unfortunate soul, and from the depths of my heart I sigh over the lot of your destruction. I weep for you, I say, miserable soul who are given over to the filth of impurity. You are to be mourned indeed with a whole fountain of tears. What a pity! "Who will give to my head waters and my eyes a fountain of tears?" And this mournful voice is not now less suitably drawn from my sobbing self than was then spoken out of the prophetic mouth. I do not bewail the stone ramparts of a city fortified by towers, not the lower buildings of a temple made by hands; I do not lament the progress of a vile people taken into the captivity of the rule of the Babylonian king. My plaint is for the noble soul made in the image and likeness of God and joined with the most precious blood of Christ. It is brighter than many buildings, certainly to be preferred to all the heights of earthly construction. Therefore I especially lament the lapse of the soul and the destruction of the temple in which Christ had resided. O eyes wear yourselves out in crying aloud, overflow the rivers full of tears, water with continuous tears my sad, mournful face! . . .

Consider, O miserable one, how much darkness weighs on your soul; notice what thick, dark blindness engulfs you. Does the fury of lust impel you to the male sex? Has the madness of lust incited you to your own kind, that is, male to male? Does a [male] goat goaded by lust, ever sometimes leap on a [male] goat? Does a ram leap on a ram, maddened with the heat of sexual union? In fact a stallion feeds calmly and peacefully with a stallion in one stall and when he sees a mare the sense of lust is immediately unleashed. Never does a bull petulantly desire a bull out of love for sexual union; never does a mule bray under the stimulant for sex with a mule. But ruined men do not fear to commit what the very brutes shrink from in horror. What is committed by the rashness of human depravity is condemned by the judgement of irrational animals.

Unmanned man, speak! Respond, effeminate man! What do you seek in a male which you cannot find in yourself? What sexual difference? What different physical lineaments? What softness? What tender, carnal attraction? What pleasant, smooth face? Let the vigour of the male appearance terrify you, I beseech you; your mind should abhor virile strength. In fact, it is the rule of natural appetite that each seek beyond himself what he cannot find within the cloister of his own faculty. Therefore, if contact with male flesh delights you, turn your hand to yourself. Know that whatever you do not find in yourself, you seek vainly in another [male] body. Woe to you, unfortunate soul, at whose ruin angels are saddened and whom the enemy insults with applause. You are made the prey of demons, the rape of the cruel, the spoils of wicked men. All your enemies open their mouths against you; they hiss and gnash their teeth. They say: "We have devoured her; this at last is the day we hoped for; we found it, we saw it."

—TRANSLATED BY PIERRE J. PAYER

on MEDIEVAL HANDBOOKS OF PENANCE

T he wages of sin is death": haunting words, even for those who don't know their context (Paul's Epistle to Romans, 6) or their continuation, which makes all the difference: "but the gift of God is eternal life through Jesus Christ our Lord." This, of course, is the crux of Christian morality, that most of what we do during the course of our lives only corrupts us, but through the love of Christ we can be saved. The implication comes rushing into the mind of the would-be sinner: Well, if I can confess my sins and be absolved, why not sin wildly, confess it all and go to heaven having lived a really fun life? The answer, at least for Catholics, is penance: our confessor will give us a certain number of prayers and punishments, depending on the level of our sins.

With this in mind, I thought it might be interesting to investigate the history of the Catholic church's views on sins of the bodily sort. So I tracked down a series of medieval "penitentials": manuals for priests on how to conduct confessions and dispense penance. Three of the penitentials I found (two from the seventh and one from the ninth century) had whole chapters on fornication, and excerpts from two of them are reprinted on the following pages. They contain a number of surprises: that "whoever sends seed into the mouth"—or whoever takes it—is committing the "worst evil"; that men are punished for homosexuality more than women; that (in one text) copulating with an animal is no greater a crime than masturbating alone; and finally, that if you don't have a wife, your penance for bestiality is cut in half. This last is a rare Christian concession to the dynamics of human desire, the implication being that if you don't have a good woman to come home to it's only natural for the milkcow to look that much more attractive.

from MEDIEVAL HANDBOOKS OF PENANCE

"The So-Called Roman Penitential"

6. If anyone commits fornication as [did] the Sodomites, he shall do penance for ten years, three of these on bread and water.

10. If anyone commits fornication by himself or with a beast of burden or with any quadruped, he shall do penance for three years; if [he has] clerical rank or a monastic vow, he shall do penance for seven years.

11. If any cleric lusts after a woman and is not able to commit the act because the woman will not comply, he shall do penance for half a year on bread and water and for a whole year abstain from wine and meat.

14. If anyone begets a child of the wife of another, that is, commits adultery and violates his neighbor's bed, he shall do penance for three years and abstain from juicy foods and from his own wife, giving in addition to the husband the price of the wife's violated honor.

15. If anyone wishes to commit adultery and cannot, that is, is not accepted, he shall do penance for forty days.

16. If anyone commits fornication with women, that is, with widows and girls, if with a widow, he shall do penance for a year; if with a girl, he shall do penance for two years.

17. If any unstained youth is joined to a virgin, if the parents are willing, she shall become his wife; nevertheless they shall do penance for one year and become man and wife.

18. If anyone commits fornication with a beast he shall do penance for one year. If he has not a wife, he shall do penance for half a year.

1. If anyone commits fornication with a virgin he shall do penance for one year. If with a married woman, he shall do penance for four years, two of these entire, and in the other two during three forty-day periods and three days a week.
2. He judged that he who often commits fornication with a man or with a beast should do penance for ten years.
3. Another judgement is that he who is joined to beasts shall do penance for fifteen years.
4. He who after his twentieth year defiles himself with a male shall do penance for fifteen years.
5. A male who commits fornication with a male shall do penance for ten years.
6. Sodomites shall do penance for seven years, and the effeminate man as an adulteress.
7. Likewise he who commits this sexual offense once shall do penance for four years. If he has been in the habit of it, as Basil says, fifteen years; but if not, one year less as a woman. If he is a boy, two years for the first offense; if he repeats it, four years.
8. If he does this "in femoribus" [between the thighs], one year, or the three forty-day periods.
9. If he defiles himself, forty days.
10. He who desires to commit fornication, but is not able, shall do penance for forty or twenty days.
11. As for boys who mutually engage in vice, he judged that they should be whipped.
12. If a woman practices vice with a woman, she shall do penance for three years.
13. If she practices solitary vice, she shall do penance for the same period.
14. The penance of a widow and of a girl is the same. She who has a husband deserves a greater penalty if she commits fornication.

15. "Qui semen in os miserit" [whoever sends seed into the mouth] shall do penance for seven years: this is the worst of evils. Elsewhere it was his judgement that both [participants in this offense] shall do penance to the end of life, or twelve years; or as above, seven.

16. If one commits fornication with his mother, he shall do penance for fifteen years and never change except on Sundays. But this so impious incest is likewise spoken of by him in another way— that he shall do penance for seven years, with perpetual pilgrimage.

17. He who commits fornication with his sister shall do penance for fifteen years in the way in which it is stated above of his mother. But this [penalty] he also elsewhere established in a canon as twelve years. Whence it is not unreasonable that the fifteen years that are written to apply to the mother.

18. The first canon determined that he who often commits fornication should do penance for ten years; a second canon, seven; but on account of the weakness of man, on deliberation they said he should do penance for three years.

19. If a brother commits fornication with a natural brother, he shall abstain from all kinds of flesh for fifteen years.

20. If a mother imitates acts of fornication with her little son, she shall abstain from flesh for three years and fast one day in the week, that is until vespers.

21. He who amuses himself with libidinous imagination shall do penance until the imagination is overcome.

22. He who loves a woman in his mind shall seek pardon from God; but if he has spoken [to her], that is, of love and friendship, but is not received by her, he shall do penance for seven days.

—TRANSLATED BY JOHN T. MCNEILL
AND HELENA M. GAMER

uch of what passes for poignancy in the lives of men are simply isolated events of particular intensity. We remember vomiting in third grade math class, hitting a game-winning home run in Little League, smoking our first cigarette, making love badly and furtively on the practice football field under winking, mocking stars. Yet perhaps these moments of seeming poignancy are simply conspicuous stoppages along the axis of what really makes life beautiful and tragic: the long lazy awakening to the realities of desire and mortality. We live and slowly learn that no rose could symbolize love if it could not also symbolize death.

I say this by way of introduction to this excerpt from Günter Grass's *The Tin Drum*. The novel is spectacular, from the opening scene of a potato farmer hiding a fugitive under her four skirts; to the visit to the liquorless "bar," the Onion Cellar, where one goes for a slice and a good cry; to the allegorical Bildung of its principal character, Oskar, the drummer boy who decided at age three to grow no more. This excerpt is Oskar's first brush with sexuality (told in both first and third person), but more than that, it is his first recognition of what normally takes years to realize: that mingled in every moment of sweetest joy is an ashy tinge of finitude.

from Günter Grass's THE TIN DRUM

It was quite beyond me why Maria . . . should whistle while removing her shoes, two high notes, two low notes, and while stripping off her socks. Whistling like the driver of a brewery truck she took off the flowery dress, whistling she hung up her petticoat over her dress, dropped her brassiere, and still without finding a tune, whistled frantically while pulling her panties, which were really gym shorts, down to her knees, letting them slip to the floor, climbing out of the rolled-up pants legs, and kicking the shorts into the corner with one foot.

Maria frightened Oskar with her hairy triangle...Rage, shame, indignation, disappointment, and a nascent half-comical, half-painful stiffening of my watering can beneath my bathing suit made me forget drum and drumsticks for...the new stick I had developed.

Oskar jumped up and flung himself on Maria. She caught him with her hair. He buried his face in it. It grew between his lips. Maria laughed and tried to pull him away. I drew more and more of her into me, looking for the source of her vanilla smell. Maria was still laughing. She even left me to her vanilla, it seemed to amuse her, for she didn't stop laughing. Only when my feet slipped and I hurt her—for I didn't let go the hair or perhaps it was the hair that didn't let me go—only when the vanilla brought tears to my eyes, only when I began to taste mushrooms or some acrid spice, in any case, something that was not vanilla, only when this earthy smell that Maria concealed behind the vanilla brought me back to the smell of the earth where Jan Brodski lay moldering and contaminated me for all time with the taste of perishability—only then did I let go.

—TRANSLATED BY RALPH MANHEIM

E very blue moon or so, when I'm feeling especially bold, I poll my various male friends in an attempt to find out if one or another of my pet sexual fantasies is "normal." By normal, I mean common or communal, or at least shared by one of the reprobates I drink 40s with. I realize there isn't (or shouldn't be) any real standard of normalcy with regard to sexual fantasies, but I still think this is a legitimate practice, if only because my suspicion is that if my fellow caitiffs have never considered something, it must be pretty original or pretty fucked up.

Now the last time I tried this, it didn't go particularly well. The fantasy under discussion was one of my all-time favorites: the hundred-foot woman. My friends already knew about my rather over-pronounced appreciation for women six feet or taller (I scale a booby-prize 5' 11"), but it seems they were rather taken aback by my wanting to be with a woman sixteen times my size. As is often the case, they looked at me as if I had a horn coming out of my forehead as I tried to explain the dynamics of such a love (the harness and rope, the swimming strokes, the oxygen tank, the clitoris the size of a beanbag). I tell you, not one of my friends endorsed this as an appealing fantasy. What simpletons! What lack of imagination! Hundred-foot women, wherever you are, whatever central African bush, undiscovered isle or aboriginal backwater you are thundering in, fear not! Mankind will find you, and you will be loved! Loved head to toe, in all your prodigy. Loved for the manhole covers of your nipples, the man-high rushes of your pubis. Loved with vigor, loved with zest (if you are able to detect it). You will be loved, yes, loved to the best of human ability, by me, your spelunking, headlamped devotee.

If, on the off chance you find the above a wee absurd, consider this excerpt from our generation's comedic goofball genius, Mark Leyner. It concerns not the allure of big, big girls, but teensy-weensy ones. It is

taken from a mock presidential news conference (a hysterical scene from his 1992 novel *Et Tu, Babe*), in which the commander in chief is being asked about the size of the first lady (she is reputed to be "the size of a letter 'o' in a magazine or newspaper"). As to the amorous implications of such a coupling, I'll let Leyner's president speak for himself, though I will say that, clever as they are, I would have thought to take a page out of Richard Gere's book...

from Mark Leyner's ET TU, BABE

Now here's where some of the controversy's been generated and I appreciate the opportunity to clear some of this up. Sex presented some very real difficulties. I had to use a jeweler's loupe in order to find her vagina and her clitoris. Utilizing a bristle from the tiny applicator used to apply solution to micro-format audio cleaning cassettes, I jury-rigged an erotic toy which I could manipulate to give her an orgasm. She then insisted that I come, too. I told her that it didn't really matter, that just experiencing her pleasure and passion was satisfying to me, but she insisted. And she insisted that she bring about my orgasm. She tried running up and down my penis in an effort to somehow generate enough friction to cause an orgasm but it didn't work and she was soon exhausted. After a rest, Barb came up with an ingenious suggestion. We cut a shoeshine cloth into a thin strip, glued the ends together to form a continuous loop, and rigged up an oblong treadmill. Barb ran in the center of the strip causing it to turn and I put my penis inside the end of the loop and the friction of the cloth buffing my erection soon did the trick.

The storyline goes like this: I was bad, real bad, then I discovered the Lord, and now it seems okay. Sounds like a classic case of Goody Two-Shoes syndrome, no? Yet despite its proselytizing, Saint Augustine's late fourth-century autobiography *The Confessions* retains its place among the übertexts of the Western canon, and for good reason. Not only does Augustine convince readers that he was just as ego-driven, pear-stealing and concupiscent as the next guy, but his eventual faith in the Lord is so strong and so compelling that it makes this reader, at least, wish he were a little less lapsed in his Catholicism.

It's important to remember the struggle involved in this most influential church father's attempts to set his life straight. Although Augustine later rails against lust and literature and all the other pleasures of his youth, he does so having felt their sway, and having realized how close he came to remaining under their influence. Instead of threatening sinners with hellfire and brimstone, Augustine cries out his own weakness, his own conflicts, and the fact that despite his human frailty the Lord came and saved him. His honesty is piercing; it reminds us that we are all weak, all conflicted, and it almost makes me wish there *was* a God who would come and save me as well.

from THE CONFESSIONS OF SAINT AUGUSTINE

I came to Carthage, where all around me in my ears a cauldron of unholy loves bubbled and sounded. I hadn't yet loved, yet I loved the idea of loving... and searched for something that I might love... For within me there was a hunger due to a lack of that inner food, which is You, my God; yet I wasn't hungry for the right sustenance and had no desire for that which is incorruptible, not because I was already filled with it, but because the more empty I was, the more I despised it. And because of this, my soul was sickly and full of ulcers, it miserably cast itself out and around, hoping to be scraped and distracted by touch and sensory input. To love then, and to be loved, seemed sweet to me—and even more so when I was able to enjoy my beloved's body. I defiled, therefore, the spring of friendship with the filth of concupiscence, and I clouded its clear waters with the hell of lust...

Thus with the burdens and baggage of this material world was I held down, but happily, as one is in sleep. And the thoughts that I directed toward Thee were like the efforts of those who want to awaken, yet remain overcome with drowsiness, and cannot free themselves... Thus when you called to me, "Waken, thou that sleeps, and arise from the dead, and Christ shall give thee light," I had no answer. And when Thou showed me all around that what You said was true, I, though convinced of its truth, could only repeat my drowsy, delirious words, "Right away, yes right away. Leave me just one more minute..." But "right away" was never right now, and my "one minute" went on for a long while... And I, a wretched young man, even more wretched than I had been in my youth, begged you for chastity, yet said, "Oh Lord, make me chaste and continent—but not yet!"

—TRANSLATED BY JACK MURNIGHAN

can't say that I'm the biggest fan of Paul Gauguin, but I know
no better title of a painting than that of his enormous masterwork, *Where Do We Come From? What Are We? Where Are We
Going?* I first saw this sprawling mural at a poignant crossroads in my
adolescent life, and the title's questions resonated through me with a
painful and probing intensity. The effect has not waned. Simply stated,
Gauguin's questions are as fundamental as you can get, and in a quick
stroke encapsulate the miracle and mystery of being sentiently alive.

Perhaps it's no wonder: in his early forties, Gauguin left France to
go to Tahiti and live among the "savages." He shed his European
clothes and mores, and developed the quasi-wisdom of the white man
gone native. I say *quasi* because the path to enlightenment is unlikely
to include an idealization of one's surroundings—yet clearly the isola-
tion and estrangement one feels living in a truly alien culture does give
us perspective on the otherwise invisible fabric of our selves. Amid his
untroubled, often embarrassing embrace of the "primitive," Gauguin
does expose a lot about the culture he came from, and even more
about himself.

All this is chronicled is Gauguin's memoir, *Noa Noa*, first published in 1897 and then again, in a somewhat different version, in 1901.
In this scene, Gauguin butts up against the very questions his painting
asks, finding his sense of identity beginning to quaver. While being led
through the forest by a naked young male, he starts to have unexpected amorous thoughts. He tries to explain it away, saying that Tahitian
culture blurs the distinction between the sexes, but, even so, he can't
help but ask himself where his illicit thoughts are coming from.
Gauguin never returns to the homoeroticism of this passage, nor to its
curious confluence of personal and societal prohibitions. It seems that
Gauguin never acted on his lust, but I sometimes wonder what held

him back: self or society? He went to Tahiti to embrace the natural and found himself desiring the "unnatural." Where do we come from? What are we? Where are we going?

from Paul Gauguin's NOA NOA

Both of us went naked, the white and blue paréo around the loins, hatchet in hand... My guide seemed to follow the trail by smell rather than by sight, for the ground was covered by a splendid confusion of plants, leaves, and flowers which wholly took possession of space.

And in this forest, this solitude, this silence were we two—he, a very young man, and I, almost an old man from whose soul many illusions had fallen and whose body was tired from countless efforts, upon whom lay the long and fatal heritage of the vices of a morally and physically corrupt society.

With the suppleness of an animal and the graceful litheness of an androgyne he walked a few paces in advance of me. And it seemed to me that I saw incarnated in him, palpitating and living, all the magnificent plant-life which surrounded us. From it in him, through him there became disengaged and emanated a powerful perfume of beauty.

Was it really a human being walking there ahead of me? Was it the native friend by whose combined simplicity and complexity I had been so attracted? Was it not rather the Forest itself, the living Forest, without sex—and yet alluring?

Among peoples that go naked, as among animals, the difference between the sexes is less accentuated than in our climates. Thanks to our cinctures and corsets we have succeeded in making an artificial being out of woman. She is an anomaly, and Nature herself, obedient to the laws of heredity, aids us in complicating and enervating her. We carefully keep her in a state of nervous weakness and muscular inferiority, and in guarding her from fatigue, we take away from her possibilities of development. Thus modeled on a bizarre ideal of slenderness to which, strangely enough, we continue to adhere, our women have nothing in common with us, and this, perhaps, may not be without grave moral and social disadvantages.

On Tahiti the breezes from forest and sea strengthen the lungs, they broaden the shoulders and hips. Neither men nor women are sheltered from the rays of the sun nor the pebbles of the seashore. Together they engage in the same tasks with the same activity or the same indolence. There is something virile in the women and something feminine in the men.

This similarity of the sexes make their relations the easier. Their continual state of nakedness has kept their minds free from the dangerous preoccupation with the "mystery" and from the excessive stress which among civilized people is laid upon the "happy accident" and the clandestine and sadistic colors of love. It has given their manners a natural innocence, a perfect purity. Man and woman are comrades, friends rather than lovers, dwelling together almost without cease, in pain as in pleasure, and even the very idea of vice is unknown to them.

In spite of all this lessening in sexual differences, why was it that there suddenly rose in the soul of a member of an old civilization, a horrible thought? Why, in all this drunkenness of lights and perfumes with its enchantment of newness and unknown mystery?

The fever throbbed in my temples and my knees shook... With tranquil eyes and ever uniform pace my companion went on. He was wholly without suspicion; I alone was bearing the burden of an evil conscience.

—TRANSLATED BY O. F. THEIS

on A CONFEDERACY OF DUNCES

𝕴t is a curious truth, long-noted by poets, that the subjects that elicit the greatest number of words are actually better addressed with brevity. I remember an issue of *Granta* from some years back dedicated to the family. On the front cover, they had quoted the terse Philip Larkin: "They fuck you up." The naughty bit below is from John Kennedy Toole's Pulitzer Prize–winning novel *A Confederacy of Dunces*, a very funny book that's hard to laugh at, at least if you know that its author committed suicide before the book was ever published. In the spirit of economy of words, then, I'll say this about death: it just ain't right. It ain't right when the young and innocent die, it ain't right when the old and wizened die and it ain't right when an unknown comic genius kills himself and never gets to see how beloved his book will become.

In *Confederacy*'s introduction, Walker Percy describes his attempts to avoid reading the manuscript, which was brought to his office at Loyola Unviversity by an older woman. The book was by her dead son, and like anyone rational, Percy was afraid of what he'd have to say to her if he actually read the thing. But he did read it, and recognized immediately the playful, goofy, tragic triumph that is Toole's novel. Thelma Toole was right to be persistent; we have her to thank that the world still has her son.

from John Kennedy Toole's A CONFEDERACY OF DUNCES

Ignatius pulled his flannel nightshirt up and looked at his bloated stomach...

"What you mumbling about in there, boy?" his mother asked through the closed door.

"I am praying," Ignatius answered angrily...

"I think it's wonderful you praying, babe. I been wondering what you do locked up in there all the time."

"Please go away!" Ignatius screamed. "You're shattering my religious ecstasy." Ignatius touched the small erection that was pointing downward into the sheet, held it, and lay still trying to decide what to do. In this position, with the red flannel nightshirt around his chest and his massive stomach sagging into the mattress, he thought somewhat sadly that after eighteen years with his hobby it had become merely a mechanical physical act stripped of the flights of fancy and invention that he had once been able to bring to it. At one time he had almost developed it into an art form, practicing the hobby with the skill and fervor of an artist and a philosopher, a scholar and a gentleman. There were still hidden in his room several accessories which he had once used, a rubber glove, a piece of fabric from a silk umbrella, a jar of Noxema. Putting them away again after it was all over had eventually grown too depressing.

Ignatius manipulated and concentrated. At last a vision appeared, the familiar figure of the large and devoted collie that had been his pet when he was in high school. "Woof!" Ignatius almost heard Rex say. "Woof! Woof! Arf!" Rex looked so lifelike. One ear drooped. He panted. The apparition jumped over a fence and chased a stick that somehow landed in the middle of Ignatius' quilt. As the tan and white fur grew closer, Ignatius' eyes dilated, crossed and closed, and he lay wanly back among his four pillows, hoping that he had some Kleenex in his room.

on "OUR SECRET"   VICTOR LAVALLE

At the beginning of her famous 1970s poem "The Moon Is Always Female," Marge Piercy asks a question many of us will have wondered about and one I find difficult to answer: "Do men always wear their sex always?" Though the answer at first seems obvious, I'm not sure...do we? Often, as a man, I fear that I do, and at those moments I have a desire to step out of my skin, to not be myself, to change my gender like a mere suit of clothes, swapping willy-nilly, one day or one hour to the next. I don't mean such a simple thing as wearing dresses, mind you, but of really knowing, Tiresias-like, what it is to be both man and woman, to see finally out of the women's eyes I spend so much time staring into.

I feel similarly about sexual preference, and here too books provide the closest rendering of the other's experience that we are likely to find. Reading Genet I come very close to believing I'm a gay man in prison, though at the same time I couldn't be more aware of just how far I am from such a condition. Reading Victor LaValle's masterfully subtle, 232-word short story "Our Secret" also makes it easy to imagine an unexpected visceral attraction to another man, a momentary blurring of the well-set lines. LaValle's character stops caring about the plumbing on the bodies described, and we, the readers, are right alongside, saying to ourselves: *I'm feeling. I'm there. It's me.* We may not be able to switch, but we can, with LaValle's help, imagine.

Victor LaValle's "OUR SECRET"

Have you ever really seen beautiful people? The women start at six feet tall. Their hair, long or short, afros or braids, is something you'd like to touch, but you know you should be afraid to. And you are.

Take Dave Anderson, whose name is vague and unassuming because if it had been lovely too maybe even his parents would have murdered him out of envy.

His eyes, if they grabbed you, were rough as you secretly wanted them to be and then rougher because you wanted to be pushed. Then he said, Hey, and his voice was only a little deep, so almost-ideal.

Hello, you replied. Then, How can I help you?

He needed something so you got it; he put out his hand and the skin was the brown of rich, sugared things that you eat in your bed when you're sure you are no good. And you bet his skin would taste like that.

Is there anything else? You asked and he shook his head real easy because he knew you'd watch quietly until he stopped. He took his time so you'd enjoy it.

Then he left a note for someone and that's how you got his name; after he left you realized your dick was hard. You repeated his name at home that night, maybe in disbelief because you swore before Tuesday that only pussy could be beautiful.

on KRISTIN LAVRANSDATTER   SIGRID UNDSET

omance—I love romance. I don't necessarily like *romances*, but I certainly like the idea. Stories of seduction, the literature of love—the very thought makes my heart go pitter-patter. But what about those pink-covered, florid, Fabio-emblazoned paperbacks with titles like *Inner Harbor* and *Savage Heat* that pass for romances these days? What's up with them? I'm a medievalist, so when I think of romance (from the Old French *romans*, meaning *story*) I think of courtly tales of mounted knights and damsels in finery in the age-old quest for honor. Over the centuries, the genre expanded to include other "romantic" tales (like the thirteenth-century *Romance of the Rose*, which I featured in my first volume of naughty bits), but still, the contemporary romance novel seems quite a step from its historical namesakes.

Or so I thought, in my ignorance. For, I confess, I'd never read a romance—I just looked down my haughty grad student nose at the lot of them. I had seen the covers, read the titles, knew their popularity, but never cracked the spine of a single Silhouette or Harlequin. Never considered it, until now.

So what was a disapproving—if underinformed—snob to do? I decided to track down a few people who could tell me where to start. So I set out on a romance odyssey...and what did I find? More than I bargained for, certainly. Not only some pretty powerful titillation (not just for schoolgirls anymore!) and some brisk, assured storytelling, but the occasional passage and scene of high literary merit. They occur amidst a mudslide of cloying prose, to be sure, but clearly that's part of the point. Like any genre, romance includes the good and the bad, the laudable and the laughable. And despite the many troubling questions that the books raise, romances make no apology. They are what they are, and, if you want my opinion, they're not all that bad.

Below are two scenes from the most critically-acclaimed work in the genre, Sigrid Undset's *Kristin Lavransdatter*, which won the Nobel Prize for Literature in 1928. Set in medieval Norway, *Kristin Lavransdatter* is a three-volume epic—it would be a conventional romance but it doesn't have a happy ending—that traces Kristin's life through the tribulations of rejecting her arranged marriage and instead marrying her lover, only to find disappointment. These two scenes read like boilerplate romance seductions, where the heroine's innocence and resistance are overcome by the hero's strength and insistence. It's a basic form, but given the popularity of the formula, it must tap into a primary source of female desire. Perhaps this accounts for the continuing popularity of the romance novel: written by and for women, they are perhaps the last place to get a good old-fashioned *ravishing* these days. *Honi soit qui mal y pense!*

from Sigrid Undset's KRISTIN LAVRANSDATTER

[First, in an herb garden . . .]

Erlend pressed the maiden to him once and asked in a whisper, "You're not afraid, are you Kristin?"

Suddenly she vaguely remembered the world outside this night—it was madness. But she was so blissfully robbed of all power. She leaned closer to the man and whispered faintly; she didn't know herself what she said . . .

She stood there with her face raised and received his kiss. He placed his hands at her temples. She thought it so wonderful to feel his fingers sinking into her hair, and then she put her hands up to his face and tried to kiss him the way he had kissed her.

When he placed his hands on her bodice and stroked her breasts, she felt as if he had laid her heart bare and then seized it; gently he parted the folds of her silk shift and kissed the place in between—heat rushed to the roots of her heart.

"You I could never hurt," whispered Erlend ... "Sleep, Kristin, sleep here with me."

[Later, in a barn, during a storm ...]

Every time there was lightning and thunder, Erlend would whisper, "Aren't you afraid, Kristin?"

"A little," she would whisper back and then press closer to him ...

The storm passed over quickly ...

"I have to go now," said Kristin.

And Erlend replied, "I suppose you do." He put his hand on her foot. "You'll get wet. You must ride, and I'll walk. Out of the forest." He gave her such a strange look.

Kristin was trembling—she thought it was because her heart was pounding so hard—and her hands were clammy and cold. When he kissed the bare skin above her knee, she tried powerlessly to push him away. Erlend raised his face for a moment, and she was suddenly reminded of a man who had once been given food at the convent—he had kissed the bread as they handed it to him. She sank back into the hay with open arms and let Erlend do as he liked.

—TRANSLATED BY TIINA NUNNALLY

on SWEET SAVAGE LOVE ROSEMARY ROGERS

kay, having just read the Sigrid Undset, do you see why I'd argue that romance novels make for pretty good reading? I wouldn't want to read them all the time, but still, all those smoking-hot virgins liquefying in the arms of their swarthy, unyielding seducers—that's excellent! I just can't believe these things are for women, at least the way I understand sexual relations. I had always thought the idea of coercing women into abandonment stemmed more from the male side of fantasy; now it seems that I might have been wrong. (Although gentlemen, need I but mention the cop/lady criminal, producer/aspiring actress or professor/student scenarios to set your hearts a-pounding? Aren't these the sugarplums of our waking and sleeping dreams? Is it only me?) A friend of mine once dreamt that he was a pagan god to whom a tribal culture would ritually sacrifice nubile virgins—and at the time, silly me, I thought that was an archetypal male fantasy! Not unlike the great high school realization that women like sex too, the very thought that my fantasies might be shared by the fairer sex implied that I wasn't quite the monster I thought I was. Who'd have thought?

Though perhaps it's a cultural thing, for certainly had I been seen with copies of *Complete Surrender* and *One Strong Man* under my arm during graduate school, I don't think I would have made many friends among the women in my department. But those days are gone, so now you're likely to catch me furtively flipping pages in the aisles of Wal-Marts everywhere. And, members of the jury, I won't be reading *Field & Stream*.

This excerpt is from one of the classics of the contemporary romance genre, Rosemary Rogers's *Sweet Savage Love*. It takes place in the Wild West amidst a constant threat of Indian attack, but I bet you never saw this on *Gunsmoke*!

Without knowing why, or what she was doing, her arms lifted, went around his neck and clung. She felt his hand move slowly and caressingly up her back, then tug impatiently at her hair, loosening it from its tidy, coiled braids. She felt her hair tumble down her shoulders, and his mouth made a burning trail from her parted lips to her earlobe. "Ginny—Ginny—" the words sounded like a groan, and a shiver of apprehension went through her as she felt his fingers start to unbutton the thin silk shirt she had worn with her riding skirt.

He mustn't—she mustn't let him—but his mouth found the hollow at the base of her throat and she made a little, helpless sound; feeling the shirt open under his hands, his fingers burn against her breast.

He held her close against him, one arm supporting her weak, trembling body, and when she would have protested against the liberties he was taking, his lips covered her open mouth, taking possession of it, stifling the words she tried to utter... Suddenly, he had bent his head, he was kissing her breasts, his tongue tracing light, teasing patterns over their sensitive peaks.

She struggled then, but only half-heartedly; both his arms imprisoned her again, she closed her eyes and let him have his way, feeling the desire to struggle or even to protest slipping away from her to be replaced by something else—something that grew like a tight, hard knot inside her belly, spreading a burning flush over her whole body...

Somewhere in the recesses of her mind was the thought: So this is how it feels—like a fever, like a coiled snake in the belly, growing, spreading heat like honey in her loins, rendering her incapable of everything but feeling...

on THE TRICKSTER: A STUDY IN AMERICAN INDIAN MYTHOLOGY

*I*t's not every day that you encounter a protagonist with a hundred-foot penis that he keeps rolled up in a box, but that's what I found when I read the Trickster myth cycle of the Winnebago Indians. These myths recount the misadventures of goofy, mischievous Trickster, a larger-than-life hero who sociologists have argued is an archetypal figure in many of the world's myths.

In the Trickster tales of the Winnebago Indians (of Wisconsin and Nebraska), Trickster is a naughty fellow with a particular affinity for his anus and penis. From among the many highlights of the variegated story, here is an excerpt dealing with Trickster's longest of schlongs and the comical uses he puts it to. I bet you never saw a magician with such a magic wand!

from Paul Radin's
THE TRICKSTER: A STUDY IN AMERICAN INDIAN MYTHOLOGY

On Trickster proceeded. As he walked along, he came to a lovely piece of land. There he sat down and soon fell asleep. After a while he woke up and found himself lying on his back without a blanket . . . His penis had become stiff and the blanket had been forced up. "That is always happening to me," he said. "My younger brother, you will lose the blanket, so bring it back." Thus he spoke to his penis. Then he took hold of it and, as he handled it, it got softer and the blanket finally fell down. Then he coiled up his penis and put it in a box. And only when he came to the end of his penis did he find his blanket. The box with the penis he carried on his back.

After that he walked down a slope and finally came to a lake. On the opposite side he saw a number of women swimming, the chief's daughter and her friends. "Now," exclaimed Trickster, "is the opportune time: now I am going to have intercourse." Thereupon he took his penis out of the box and addressed it, "My younger brother, you are going after the chief's daughter. Pass her friends, but see that you lodge squarely in her, the chief's daughter." Thus speaking he dispatched it. It went sliding on the surface of the water. "Younger brother, come back, come back! You will scare them away if you approach in that manner!" So he pulled his penis back, tied a stone around its neck, and sent it out again. This time it dropped to the bottom of the lake. Again he pulled it back, took another stone, smaller in size, and attached it to its neck. Soon he sent it forth again. It slid along the water, creating waves as it passed along. "Brother, come back, come back! You will drive the women away if you create waves like that." So he tried a fourth time. This time he got a stone, just the right size and just the right weight, and attached it to its neck. When he dispatched it, this time it went directly towards the designated place. It passed and just barely touched the friends of the chief's daughter. They saw it and cried out, "Come out of the water, quick!" The chief's daughter was the last one on the bank and could not get away, so the penis lodged squarely in her. Her friends came back and tried to pull it out, but to no avail. They could do absolutely nothing. Then the men who had the reputation for being strong were called and tried it but they, too, could not move it. Finally they all gave up. Then one of them said, "There is an old woman around here who knows many things. Let us go and see her." So they went and got her and brought her to the place where this was happening. When she came there she recognized immediately what was taking place. "Why, this is First-born, Trickster. The chief's daughter is having intercourse and you are all annoying her." Thereupon she went out, got an awl, and straddling the penis, worked the awl into it a number of times, singing as she did so, "First-born, if it is you, pull it out! Pull it out!"

Thus she sang. Suddenly in the midst of her singing, the penis was jerked out and the old woman was thrown a great distance. As she stood there bewildered, Trickster, from across the lake laughed loudly at her. "That old naughty woman! Why is she doing this when I am trying to have intercourse? Now she has spoiled all the pleasure."

on MANTISSA

JOHN FOWLES

he scenario is intriguing: a man who has lost his memory lies in a futuristic hospital awaiting treatment. The assumption behind the cure he's about to receive is that memory is linked to the ego, and what impedes a patient's recovery is the intervention of the superego. The only way around the barrier is to stimulate the id, and the natural means, so the logic goes, is to get the patient off. Thus begins John Fowles's interesting, but very self-reflexive, very 1980s novel, *Mantissa*.

While there are other scenes in Fowles's novels that could be used for naughty bits, *Mantissa* provides not only a rather sexy base scenario, but a curious interplay of desire, coercion and fantasy. The amnesic patient, Mr. Greene, is resistant to the treatment; he wants to hold on to his morality (he's married, doesn't want to cheat, doesn't want to have sex with a perfect stranger, etc.) and tries to keep from getting aroused. But the more he resists, the more the doctor and nurse redouble their efforts. The reader, who is made to be complicit in the fantasy, can't help but imagine himself in this position, trying not to get aroused in hopes that the practitioners will proceed to even more arousing "treatments." The vicarious thrill of holding back, holding back, holding back until you get exactly what you want: now that's erotic! Fowles's short scene demonstrates that even male sexual desire is subject to the push-and-pull dynamics of deferral and inversion and that, despite some popular misconceptions, some male behaviors have evolved since the Neanderthal days.

from John Fowles's MANTISSA

"Give me your right hand, Mr. Green."

Frozen, he did nothing, but the doctor took the hand from beneath his head and led it upwards. It touched a bare breast. Once more shocked and horrified, he opened his eyes. Dr. Delfie was leaning over him, with the white tunic open, staring at the wall above his head, as if she were doing no more than taking his pulse. His hand was led to her other breast.

"What are you doing?"

She did not look down. "Please don't talk, Mr. Green. I want you to concentrate on tactile sensation." ...

She leaned across him, supporting herself on either side of the pillow. "Now both hands. Anywhere you like."

"I can't. I don't know you from Adam." ...

"You're in a hospital, for heaven's sake. There's nothing personal in this. Nurse and I are simply carrying out standard practice. All we ask is a little cooperation. Nurse?"

"Still negative doctor." ...

He sought for something in her eyes: the faintest trace of humour, of irony, of humanity even. But there was none. She was implacably indifferent to his scruples, his modesty, his sense of decorum. In the end he shut his eyes and found the breasts again, then felt cautiously upwards to the delicate throat, to the angles where the neck joined the shoulders; then down to the breasts again, to the sides, the curved indent of the waist, with the light linen of the opened tunic on the backs of his hands...

After a moment, Dr. Delfie crouched over him. A nipple touched his lips, then again, and the scent of the myrtle-flowers was stronger, evoking in some lost recess of mind sunlit slopes above azure seas. He opened his eyes, in twilight now, tented beneath the sides of the tunic; once more he was invited to suckle the insistent breast. He twisted his head to one side.

"Brothel."

"Excellent. Anything that spurs your libido."

"You're no doctor."

"Bonds. A whip. Black leather. Whatever you fancy."

"This is monstrous." ...

"You're only getting this because you're a private patient, Mr. Green."

on "LOVE MADE IN THE FIRST AGE: TO CHLORIS"

RICHARD LOVELACE

Perhaps had I been cut of a nobler cloth the pleasures of the flesh would be of less consequence to me. Philosophy or politics would rule the day, and the vagaries of romance would not waylay my every thought. But, alas, I am a man of mere heart and bone, wont to turn my head at a passing beauty or linger over the trivialities of tea and toe polish. It is for this reason that I read Lovelace and feel at ease in his world of playful love. For even in the midst of the political turmoil of seventeenth-century England, Lovelace wrote of lust and longing, inking his quill not for heads of state, but for the Lucastas and the Altheas, the Chlorises and the Amaranthas.

Nor, apparently, were the Amaranthas in short supply. In one poem, Lovelace responds to his mistress' concerns about his fidelity in truly exemplary fashion: "Lady it is already morn, / And 'twas last night I swore to thee / That fond impossibility. / Have I not loved thee much and long / A tedious twelve hours' space?" I ask you, is there a terser manifesto of a rollin' stone? And while Muddy Waters promised five minutes, Lovelace claims twelve hours, leading me to wonder what more a woman could want—except, of course, not to be considered tedious.

In the poem here, however, the dynamic is a little different. As this Chloris apparently did not take good Richard up on his offers, he inundates her with images of the golden age of romance that are meant to get her all worked up. But in the last lines we see that it's the author himself who gets jazzed from the descriptions, so much so that he loses whatever interest he had in the girl. Given the chance, she didn't take it, and Lovelace finds another lover. Perhaps Miss Chloris would have done well to remember that even with pen in hand, one hand remains free.

from Richard Lovelace's
"LOVE MADE IN THE FIRST AGE: TO CHLORIS"

In the nativity of time,
Chloris, it was not thought a crime
In direct Hebrew for to woo...
Thrice happy was that golden age...
When cursed "No" stained no maid's bliss,
And all discourse was summed in "Yes,"
And nought forbidden, but to forbid.
Love then unstinted, Love did sip,
And cherries plucked fresh from the lip,
On cheeks and roses free he fed;
Lasses like Autumn plums did drop,
And lads, indifferently did crop
A flower, and a maidenhead.
Then unconfined each did tipple
Wine from the bunch, milk from the nipple,
Paps tractable as udders were;
Then equally the wholesome jellies,
Were squeezed from olive trees, and bellies,
Nor suits of trespass did they fear...
Naked as their own innocence,
And unembroidered from offense
They went, above poor riches, gay;
On softer than the cignet's down,
In beds they tumbled of their own;
For each within the other lay.
Thus did they live: thus did they love,
Repeating only joys above;
And angels were, but with clothes on,
Which they would put off cheerfully,
To bathe them in the galaxy,
Then gird them with the heavenly zone.

Now, Chloris, miserably crave
The offered bliss you would not have;
Which evermore I must deny,
Whilst ravished with these noble dreams,
And crowned with mine own soft beams,
Enjoying of myself I lie.

on "GAVRILIADA"   ALEXANDER PUSHKIN

𝔍 don't know if you're one of those types who gets really sad and offended when a catalog comes out that perfectly captures your aesthetic. I am. Every time some Pottery Republic releases a new tartan-boxer/martini-set gift pack, I am both thrilled and appalled. What could be better? But how did they know? Have I become such an identifiable social type, so prefab a demographic that I fall perfectly into their marketing department's nefarious plans? It appears so.

But what if it's not your clothing preferences or interior decor that's being anticipated, but your very ethos, your *episteme*, your *Weltanschauung*? What then—triumph or despair? Finally, you are understood, someone gets it, you can be pinned down with a single word. But one word? Only one? It's scary, but this is the situation I found myself in when I first came across that eminently applicable term, *Weltschmerz*. Weltschmerz: a kind of sentimental melancholy caused by comparing the actual world to the ideal worlds that you dream up. Hamlet suffered from it; Pushkin's Eugene Onegin as well; clearly I and maybe you suffer from it too. For that's all I think about, really: the feeling of having known love and evermore feeling its absence. Of having tasted perfection and not being able to forget it, even if it is never tasted again. Of imagining the compassion you could bring to the world and having it go untapped. In the words of Dante's Francesca: "There is no greater sorrow than to remember days of joy in days of pain"; for one suffering from Weltschmerz, all days are painful compared to the joyful ones you know could exist, the joy you could feel in your heart, the joy that should be. It's a bitter pill, desire. Tantalus suffers more than Sisyphus, Heloise more than Joan of Arc.

And what, then, is the antidote? How does one proceed? Humor is the only hope, surely. And thus the same mind that created Onegin, in all his disillusion, creates "Gavriliada," a raucous rewriting of the Immaculate Conception. In Pushkin's version, God chooses Mary because she's smoking hot and under-serviced by her husband. Claiming an "Armenian" source, Pushkin gives the Virgin Mother more action in an afternoon than most saints get their whole lives. Ah, finally a religion I can believe in! Blasphemy never had it so good.

Note: Okay, I realize this "bit" is more than bite-sized, but trust me, it's worth it. Where else can you find a poem where the Virgin Mary is an untended-to wife; the archangel Gabriel is God's begrudging procurer; Satan argues on behalf of sex (and then has it with Mary); Gabriel and Satan fight (with the former winning only by biting the latter on the dick); Gabriel only gets to second base with Mary; and then finally God appears as a dove and pecks Mary on the clit? Now that's some poem! And that, my friends, is classic nasty...

from Alexander Pushkin's "GAVRILIADA"

In stilly fields, far from Jerusalem,
Far from those sports and young philanderers,
Bred up by Satan but to ruin us,
A gentle beauty, seen as yet none,
And not capricious, lived her tranquil life.
Her husband was a man respectable
And old. A carpenter and joiner he,
The real workman in the town,
And day and night having so much to do,
Now with his level, now with faithful saw,
He little tasted of these charms he owned.
The hidden flower, as though by ancient fate
To some high other honor designate,
Upon its little stem did not unfold.

The languid man with his old sprinkling pot
Gazed on the flower at times, but sprinkled not.
He lived, a father, with his tender bride;
He fed her well—and nothing else beside.
But from just heaven in those days of old,
The All-highest God inclined a gracious eye
Upon the comely shape of his hand-maiden,
The bosom sweetly pure—and feeling heat,
In the depth of his all-wisdom he ordained
To bless the blameless garden thus forgotten,
And make it fertile with mysterious fruit.
Then summoning his favorite, Gabriel,
He told him in straight prose about his love.
The church somewhat suppressed their conversation,
The evangelist perhaps was negligent,
But following an Armenian tradition
Gabriel received the praise of God,
Was noted tactful and intelligent,
And down to Mary in the twilight sent.
He would have liked, I judge, a different honor.
He had as an ambassador been true,
Delivered documents, brought back the news—
All well enough, but still he had pride!
He veiled his inward thought: professed that God
No safer herald-angel had, nor surer—
To put it in our earthly tongue—procurer.
But now the old fiend, Satan, slumbered not.
He heard while sauntering among the stars,
That God had this young Jewess in his eye,
A sweetheart who should save our tottering race
From everlasting torment in his hell.
The fiend was irritated—and was active.
The All-Highest meanwhile, sitting in the sky

In sweet despondency, forgot the world,
Which tripped without him on its own sweet way.
But Mary, look! A most exquisite snake!
With lovely luring scales and shiny colors!
There in the branches right above your head!
And listen too! "Beloved of heaven," he says,
"Fly not—I am your most obedient slave!"
Can it be possible? A miracle!
Who speaks these words of accent soft and level?
Whose is that oily voice? Of course! The Devil.
The wily beast unwound his rattling tail;
He arched his neck up slowly like a yoke,
And slid right down in front of gentle Mary.
Breathing hot wishes in her breast, he said:
"Young Eve like you
Was modest in her garden, clever, kind,
But without love she bloomed in melancholy.
Alone, and eye to eye, the man, the maid,
Along the shore of Eden's shining waters,
Dragged out in quietness a resting life.
A bore to them the day's monotony:
The shady grove, their youth, their idleness—
Nothing, awakened in their bodies love.
With hand in hand they walked, existed, ate.
They yawned by daytime, and by night they held
No festivals of passion, knew no joys...
What say you? Is not that old Hebrew God
A tyrant, glum, unjust and stubborn, who
Loved Adam's girl and kept her for himself?
And where's the honor there? Where is the fun?
I just resolved, in spite of the Creator,
To break this dreadful sleep of man and maid.
No doubt you've often heard how it all happened:

Two apples, hanging in the wondrous bough,
A happy sign, a symbol of love's summons,
Made clear to her vague imaginings,
Awakened in her breast a vague desire.
She knew her beauty, knew the bliss of it,
The trembling heart, the lover's nakedness.
I saw them—O, I saw the exquisite
Beginnings of my science, love! Away
Into the little thicket wood they walked.
Their glances quickly wandered, and their hands.
Between the darling legs of his young love,
Embarrassed, mute and awkward, Adam sought
The lovely drunken ravishment of bliss:
He put his question to the source of joy,
And seething to the deeps, he lost himself.
And Eve, unfearful of the wrath of God,
All flame, with hair thrown wide, and lips that barely,
Barely moved to answer Adam's lips,
And tears of love, and love's unconsciousness,
Lay in the palm-tree's shadow—and young earth
Strewed with her brightest blossoms their young love."
And suddenly the serpent disappeared.
A beauteous youth was sitting at her feet,
And light that streamed upon her from his eyes
In silence asked most eloquently something.
With one hand he presents to her a flower,
The other crumples back her simple linen,
Steals up hastily beneath her gown,
And the light finger touches playfully
The tender mysteries. It all seemed new
And wonderful to Mary, and ingenious.
And blushes that were not the blush of shame
Played forth upon her beauty virginal,

And languid heat and an impatient sighing
Lifted the young lovely breast of Mary.
She did not speak: she suddenly lost strength,
And closed her glistening eyes—a simple lass!
Inclining toward her Fiend her gentle head,
She cried but "Ah!" and fell back on the grass.
And suddenly above the wearied maid,
Cavorting on a sporting wing, appears
Young Gabriel, love's envoy, son of Heaven!
At sight of him our beauty hid her eyes.
The Accursed spoke, and frowning, hot with hate,
Biting his lip and sideways glowering,
He struck the Archangel Gabriel in the teeth.
The Angel yelled; he tottered; his left knee
Went down to earth; but suddenly he rose
And, filled with unexpected heat, he swung
And sent the Fiend a right hook to the jaw.
The Devil groaned; he paled; they leaped and clinched,
And knit together, rolled across the meadow.
When just by luck the squirming Gabriel grinned
And set his teeth into that fatal spot
(Superfluous in most all kinds of battle)
The haughty limb wherewith the Devil sinned.
Yelling for mercy, the Accursed fell,
And staggered dimly down the road to hell.
Breathless upon this battle Mary stared;
And the victor turned to her with grace.
He knelt before her, gently pressed
Her hand; she dropped her eyes and Gabriel kissed her.
She blushed confusedly, but stayed quite still;
And Gabriel made bold to touch her breast.
"Leave me alone!" she whispered. And with this
The last faint groan of innocence

Was stifled in a mighty angel's kiss.
Already Gabriel with tidings fair
Flies home to heaven: God is waiting there.
"Well, what's the news?" he says.
Says Gabriel:
"I did all that I could—I sounded her."
"And she?"
"She's willing."
In her small corner, drunk with memory,
Our Mary rests upon a rumpled sheet.
Her body burns with bliss and with desire.
New heat already in her youthful breast,
She whispers in the darkness, "Gabriel!"
Another gift is waiting for his love.
She moves away the covers with her foot,
And downward gives a little happy smile.
She is complacent in her nakedness,
With her own grace and loveliness surprised.
And in a tender-thoughtful midnight spell
She sins a little, charming-languidly.
She drinks the cup of tranquil consolation.
I hear you laugh, O crafty Fiend in hell!
But look! Darts in the window from above
On snow-white wings a little fluffy dove!
He circles, tries a happy tune—and flap!—
He lights right in the languid maiden's lap!
Under the little linen gown he hustles,
He pecks her rose, and squirms about, and rustles,
With little claw and little beak he bustles.
'Tis He—precisely He!—and Mary guessed
That someone else was in the birdie's breast.
Squeezing her knees together tight, she screamed,
She sighed, prayed, trembled, wept, but seemed

Unable to forestall the little dove.
He cooed and quivered in the heat of love,
Then fell in rapture, lightly slumbering,
Love's blossom shielded by his downy wing.
At last the little pigeon flew away.
And weary Mary thought: What can I say!
One, two and three—that's quite the revel,
To have all on a single summer day
The Deity, an Angel, and the Devil!

—TRANSLATED BY MAX EASTMAN,
MODIFIED SLIGHTLY BY JACK MURNIGHAN

CREDITS